4大高分關鍵，能不假思索回答，
讓「考官秒懂」、應考「獲取高分」

2

陳幸美 ◎著

高分關鍵1：熟悉必考雅思口說話題

由必考語庫來練習，以最完備的狀態來應考，大幅降低因應試時對考題的不確定感或緊張所引起的失分。

高分關鍵2：提升英語聊天續航力

Part 1量身打造一問三答單元，熟悉三種思路後融入自己的回答，面對考官時能靈活應答，不怕無話可說。

高分關鍵3：激發創意潛能

Part 2規劃語庫擴充小單元，一種話題8種回答，學習＋答題創意度成果X8，用字遣詞絕不會重覆！

高分關鍵4：充滿native speaker的活力、臨場反應力和自信

Part 3嚴選討論話題，即刻提升臨場反應力，答題流暢又活潑，以最符合英美人士的思維＋用語應戰。

雅思口試應該是很多人最頭痛的一關，見到考官緊張是難免的。其實口試的問題都是與考生本身相關，應考時考生可以把自己想成是剛轉學到新學校或是剛進公司的新人，考官則是新學校或是新公司的老鳥。以認識新朋友聊天的方式來回答問題，所以答案及內容一定不會太精簡，就算只是單純是與非的問題，也要對回答多加說明。

口試的回答沒有所謂的正確答案因為每個人的背景不同，把話講清楚才是得分的關鍵，用字遣詞盡量選用自己熟悉的字。與其死背答案不如學習如何有條有理的將自己的立場，生活體驗講清楚說明白。筆者用自然的口吻，接近生活化的回答方式供讀者發想。有時候有趣，令人印象深刻的答案有時候反而讓人耳目一新，所以不需要太拘束。

陳幸美

許多人在準備雅思考試上費了不少心思，在聽力或閱讀單項上透過補習等不斷衝高到 8 分、8.5 分、9 分，以期許能拉高平均分數到 7 分甚至是 7.5 分，最後儘管申請到了理想學校，但在口說或寫作單項上卻出現 6 分或 6.5 分的成績。這些跡象似乎也透漏著在口說或寫作單項要拿到 7 分以上其實不太容易。

許多從小到大英語成績優異的學習者，似乎也對於準備雅思考試備感困惑。因為我們都熟悉了填鴨式、記憶式的學習，在極重本身邏輯表達、分析的口試或寫作上，像隻蹣跚的山羊，疲憊著走著，卻似乎看不到一道希望之光。

而這本雅思口說書將考生所困惑之處，全列入考量。其實不管所學習的語言為何，考官或聽者能立即了解你所傳達的意思，就是最好的表達。其中當然還牽涉到語言表達是否道地、語言使用、口語流利程度、發音等等。本書規劃的「一問三答」、「PART 2 口說回答」和「PART 3 口說回答」就將考生是否能以語意連貫的方式、道地的傳達訊息和在面對考官詢問時能從容應答列入考量。每個答案均非坊間模板所能比擬，相信考生在研讀後，必能脱胎換骨獲取理想成績。

編輯部敬上

Contents 目次

Part 1 雅思口語第一部分

・地點類

・人物類

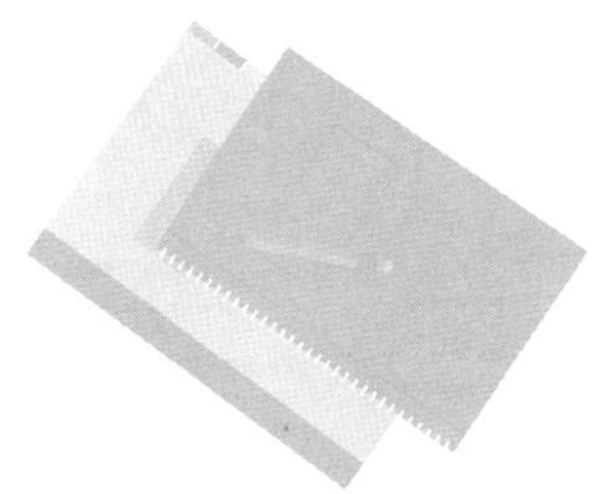

· 事件類

· 物品類

Part 2 雅思口語第二部分

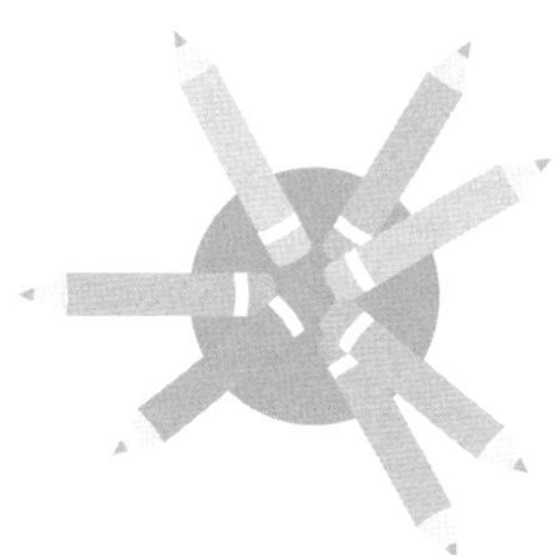

Part 3 雅思口語第三部分

雅思口語第一部分

學習進度表

- 地點類

☐ Unit 01 Hometown 家鄉
☐ Unit 02 Housing 房屋
☐ Unit 03 Building 建築物
☐ Unit 04 Restaurant 餐廳
☐ Unit 05 Park 公園
☐ Unit 06 Museum 博物館
☐ Unit 07 Hotel 飯店
☐ Unit 08 Sport Center 活動中心
☐ Unit 09 Outdoor place 戶外地點

- 人物類

☐ Unit 10 Neighbour 鄰居
☐ Unit 11 Teacher 老師
☐ Unit 12 Ideal partner理想情人
☐ Unit 13 Friend 朋友
☐ Unit 14 Child 小孩
☐ Unit 15 Animal 動物
☐ Unit 16 Relatives 親戚

- 事件類

☐ Unit 17 Weather/Season 天氣/季節
☐ Unit 18 School days 求學生涯
☐ Unit 19 Talent 才藝
☐ Unit 20 Driving 開車
☐ Unit 21 Birthday 生日
☐ Unit 22 Accident 意外
☐ Unit 23 Work/study 工作 / 求學
☐ Unit 24 Travel 旅遊
☐ Unit 25 Sport event 運動比賽
☐ Unit 26 Weekend/Free time 周末/休閒

- 物品類

☐ Unit 27 Colour 顏色
☐ Unit 28 Computer 電腦
☐ Unit 29 Movie 電影
☐ Unit 30 Vehicle 交通工具
☐ Unit 31 Song 歌曲
☐ Unit 32 Photograph 照片
☐ Unit 33 TV program 電視節目
☐ Unit 34 Fashion/ Clothing 穿著
☐ Unit 35 Food 食物
☐ Unit 36 Game 遊戲

是否能於考場中獲取理想成績?

★ 完成 16 單元 ▸ 可能
★ 完成 27 單元 ▸ 較有可能
★ 完成 36 單元 ▸ 一定可以

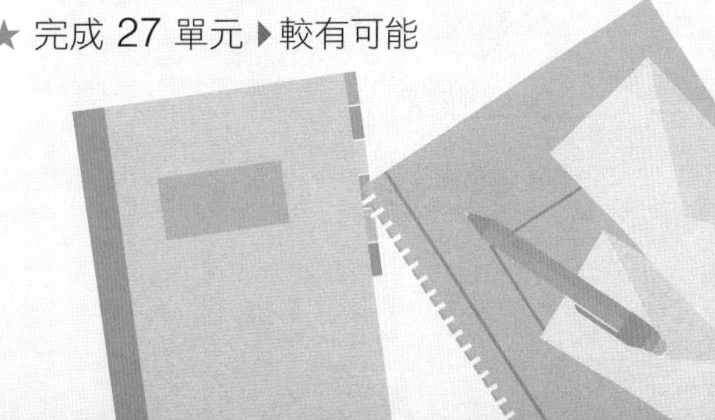

Hometown

家鄉

家鄉可以涵蓋的部分很廣，從地理位置上的氣候來說又可以分為熱帶（tropical）、亞熱帶（semi-tropical）。台灣最有可能產生天災的季節是颱風季（typhoon season）而颱風所產生的問題有炎熱潮濕（hot and humid）、淹水（flood）、土石流（landslide）。從台灣特有的景觀來切入的話，可以介紹停紅燈時滿坑滿谷的摩托車（scooter）、市區的高樓大廈（high risers）、郊區的果園（orchard）還有田間偶然出現的墳地（cemetery）。由地方特色或美景上來說，也可以介紹斷崖（cliff）、溪流（creek）、濕地（wet land）、水庫（reservoir）、漁村（fishing village）、溫泉（hot spring）、夜市（night market），保護區（conservation area）等等。

雅思主題字彙表

❶ 熱帶	tropical
❷ 亞熱帶	semi-tropical
❸ 颱風季	typhoon season

❹ 炎熱潮濕	hot and humid
❺ 淹水	flood
❻ 土石流	landslide
❼ 摩托車	scooter
❽ 高樓大廈	high risers
❾ 果園	orchard
❿ 墳地	cemetery
⓫ 斷崖	cliff
⓬ 溪流	creek
⓭ 濕地	wet land
⓮ 水庫	reservoir
⓯ 漁村	fishing village
⓰ 溫泉	hot spring
⓱ 夜市	night market
⓲ 保護區	conservation area
⓳ 歷史背景	historical background
⓴ 原住民	aboriginal
㉑ 部落/族群	tribe

一問三答

Can you tell me something about your hometown?

可以告訴有關你家鄉的一些事嗎?

Josh ▸ During my upbringing, I was lucky enough to be raised in Heng Chuan, a small town of the southern end of Taiwan right by the famous beach area called Kenting. Like every other kid growing up in the area, I spent a lot of time under the sun doing surfing and snorkeling. You don't get that kind of lifestyle elsewhere!

喬許 ▸ 我很幸運的我小時候在恆春長大，恆春是台灣南邊的一個小鎮，就在有名的墾丁海域旁邊。每個恆春長大的小孩從小就花很多時間在戶外衝浪和浮潛，我也不例外。別的地方可找不到這種生活方式呢!

Abby ▸ I was born in Kaohsiung, the 2nd largest city located in southern Taiwan. I have always been a city girl, and I love the hustle and bustle, and Kaohsiung city offers exactly that. There are numbers of famous

night markets adjacent to charming beaches nearby. Being a tropical city, summer in Kaohsiung gets quite brutal, but winter is normally very mild, nice, and pleasant.

艾比 ▸ 我在南台灣的高雄出生，高雄市台灣的第二大城市。我從小就是個城市女孩，我喜歡熱鬧的感覺，而高雄就是這樣的地方。高雄有一些有名的夜市，也很靠近迷人的海灘。因為高雄位於熱帶，夏天可是熱得很，但是冬天通常也不太冷，很舒適怡人。

Cameron ▸ I was born in Chia-yi before my family moved to Taipei. Chia-yi is a small town south of Taichung. Cha-yi is famous for the turkey on rice and the beautiful sun rise in Ali Mountain, one of the major attractions in Central Taiwan. One thing people didn't realize about Chia-Yi is how cold it gets in winter because we get cold breezes from the mountains.

卡麥倫 ▸ 在我家搬來台北之前，我是在嘉義出生的。嘉義是台中南邊的一個地方。嘉義有名的火雞肉飯還有迷人的阿里山日出，那可是中台灣有名的景點。大家通常不知道嘉義的冬天非常的冷，因為有山區的寒風吹下來。

Housing

房屋

台灣早期的傳統式房屋種類有平房（single story building）、連排透天厝（town house）等，但隨著都市化等因素，其他形式的建築像是電梯大樓住宅（apartment）也開始林立，其中公寓中每單位稱為（unit），有些大樓也推出套房（studio）租售，提供給單身族。在國外幾乎是獨棟包含含前後院的房子（cottage）和別墅（mansion）等等。有的還附有後院的戶外用餐區（alfresco），甚至於頂樓陽台（balcony）上附有省電裝置如太陽能板（solar power），有些家庭主婦甚至將廚房是否附有烤箱（oven）或屋外是否有雙車庫（double garage）也納入考量，不過最重要的還是準備頭期款（down payment），評估能府負擔房貸（mortgage）、月付金額（repayment），若是再都市工作則需考量若租賃（lease）則需要考量押金（bond）、租金（rent）金額。

雅思主題字彙表

❶ 平房	Single story building
❷ 連排透天厝	town house

③ 電梯大樓住宅	apartment
④ 公寓單位	unit/Flat
⑤ 套房	studio/ Suite
⑥ 別墅	mansion
⑦ 獨棟含前後院的房子	cottage
⑧ 烤箱	oven
⑨ 雙車庫	double garage
⑩ 太陽能板	solar power
⑪ 陽台	balcony
⑫ 後院的戶外用餐區	alfresco
⑬ 頭期款	down payment
⑭ 房貸	mortgage
⑮ 月付金額	repayment
⑯ 租賃	lease
⑰ 押金	bond
⑱ 租金	rent
⑲ 電梯	lift
⑳ 樓梯間	staircase

一問三答

What kind of housing do you have?

你家裡是住怎樣的房子？

Josh ▸ We have a three-bedroom apartment in a 15 story building. There is little space in the apartment itself, but we do have a large public area with an outdoor communal pool and an indoor gym. I love going down for a swim on Saturday afternoon because the hot chick from 12 B likes to hang out by the pool.

喬許 ▸ 我們家在一棟 15 樓的大樓裡，是一間三房的單位。屋子裡的空間不是很大，可是公共區域倒是蠻大的，有個公用的室外游泳池還有室內的健身房。我最喜歡星期六下午去游泳因為 12 樓 B 座的美眉都是那個時候去。

Abby ▸ Currently, I am renting the top floor out from a lady who owns a 3 story town house right next to Xin-dian MRT station. It is quite an old building, but the rent is surprisingly cheap compared with central Tai-

pei. The decoration of the house is very dated, and there are a few issues with the plumbing, but as long as it is not haunted, I can live with a few leaking pipes.

艾比 ▸ 目前我跟我的房東太太承租一棟三層樓透天厝的頂樓，就在新店捷運站旁邊。那是一棟很舊的房子，可是租金跟台北市中心比起來真的便宜很多。房子的裝飾很過時，而且家裡也有管線漏水的問題，可是只要沒有鬧鬼，我是不太介意滴水的問題啦。

Cameron ▸ Mum and Dad worked really hard to own our flat. It is on the 5th floor, but there is no lift in the building. We are planning to move to somewhere on the ground floor because my mum's got arthritis and her knees are getting worn out. Walking up and down the stairs everyday is killing her.

卡麥倫 ▸ 我爸媽很辛苦地買下我們住的公寓，公寓位在 5 樓可是沒有電梯。我們在想是不是要找個位在一樓的地方搬，因為我媽有關節炎，她的膝蓋快不行了，每天要走樓梯爬上爬下真的要她的命。

Building

建築物

建築物的種類可以從地標（landmark）說起，例如:摩天大樓（skyscraper）、古蹟（historical building）、教堂（church）、佛寺（temple）、巨蛋（superdome）、體育館（stadium）或是特殊的工廠，例如水泥工廠（cement factory）或是煉油廠（oil refinery）。也可以從代表國家的建築物來發想，例如總統府（presidential hall）、市政府（city hall） 等等。或是換個角度從特殊的外觀設計切入，例如:窗戶的形狀（shape）、頂樓（rooftop）的設施、戶外或高樓觀景台（viewing platform）、走道（hallway）、人造水池（water feature）等等。而選擇節能減碳（reduce carbon footprint）的建材（building material）的種類的設計也是一種趨勢。

雅思主題字彙表

❶ 地標	landmark
❷ 摩天大樓	skyscraper
❸ 古蹟	historical building

④ 教堂	church
⑤ 佛寺	temple
⑥ 總統府	presidential hall
⑦ 巨蛋	superdome
⑧ 體育館	stadium
⑨ 水泥工廠	cement factory
⑩ 煉油廠	oil refinery
⑪ 形狀	shape
⑫ 頂樓	rooftop
⑬ 觀景台	viewing platform
⑭ 建材	building material
⑮ 走道	hallway
⑯ 人造水池	water feature
⑰ 節能減碳	reduce carbon footprint
⑱ 裝飾牆	feature wall
⑲ 玻璃帷幕	architectural glass
⑳ 人造草皮	artificial lawn

一問三答

Can you recommend an interesting building in your home country to the tourist?

能推薦我你國家的一棟建築物給觀光客?

Josh ▸ Sure thing! It would have to be the 85 Sky Tower in Kaohsiung. It is more than just an ordinary skyscraper. It is a shape of a castle to be exact and situated in the Kaohsiung harbour. The outside architectural glasses reflect the view of the harbour. It looks amazing during sunset. Nothing can really top that!

喬許 ▸ 當然可以!我會推薦高雄的 85 大樓，它跟一般的摩天大廈不同，它的外觀像一座城堡而且坐落在高雄港邊。外觀的玻璃帷幕反射著海港的景觀，日落的時候看起來真是美呆了! 沒有什麼比那更好了!

Abby ▸ It might not be everyone's cup of tea, but I will recommend the waste incinerator in Bei-Tuo, Taipei. The incinerator is a 150 meters tall chimney with a re-

volving restaurant on the roof top and a viewing platform. I will recommend the visitors to have a meal in the restaurant as long as they can get over the idea of having a meal on top of piles of rubbish.

艾比 ▸ 我想推薦的建築可能有些人沒辦法接受，那就是北投的垃圾焚化爐。它的外觀像個 150 公尺高的煙囪，頂樓卻有個旋轉餐廳還有觀景台。如果大家不排斥坐在滿坑滿谷的垃圾上吃的東西的話，那我會建議旋轉餐廳用個餐。

Cameron ▸ Yes, the first thing to come to mind is the Lan Yang Museum located in Yi-Lan county. What makes it interesting is, it looks like a tilted building and half of it has sunken into the lakc, you think you are seeing the other half that is emerged on the water. The design is so clever, and I have never seen anything else like it.

卡麥倫 ▸ 可以，我第一個想到的建築物是位在宜蘭的蘭陽博物館。它最有趣的地方是建築物本身看起來像一座半倒的建築，而其中一半沉在湖裡。你會覺得你看到的是浮出水面的一半，它的設計真的很特殊，我從來沒有看過這樣子的設計。

Restaurant

餐廳

以種類來區分可以分成主題餐廳（theme restaurant）、庭園餐廳（outdoor café），自助餐廳（buffet restaurant/ all-you-can-eat restaurant）、素食餐廳（vegetarian restaurant）、親子餐廳（family restaurant）、無菸餐廳（smoke-free restaurant）、速食餐廳（fast food restaurant）等等。跳開一般餐廳的標準來說，近年來百貨公司美食區（food court）也很受歡迎、或是夜市小吃攤（hawker food stall）也能獲選米其林星級的榮譽。點餐時在特殊時段會有不同的套餐（combo）、或是可以單點（a lar Carte/ on its own）、前菜（entrée）、主餐（main）之類。有些主詞餐廳會有特殊的座位設計，例如情人座（lover's seat）、固定式的長桌沙發座（booth）、包廂（private room）等等，包廂可能會有低消（minimum charge）的限制。

雅思主題字彙表

❶ 主題餐廳	theme restaurant
❷ 庭園餐廳	outdoor café

③ 自助餐廳	buffet restaurant / all-you-can-eat restaurant
④ 素食餐廳	vegetarian restaurant
⑤ 親子餐廳	family restaurant
⑥ 無菸餐廳	smoke-free restaurant
⑦ 速食餐廳	fast food restaurant
⑧ 百貨公司美食區	food court
⑨ 夜市小吃攤	hawker food stall
⑩ 套餐	combo
⑪ 單點	a lar Carte / on its own
⑫ 前菜	entrée
⑬ 主餐	main
⑭ 情人座	lover's seat
⑮ 固定式的長桌沙發座	booth
⑯ 包廂	private room
⑰ 低消	minimum charge
⑱ 外燴	catering
⑲ 外帶	takeaway/To go
⑳ 各付各的	go Dutch / split bills

一問三答

Q4 What is your favourite restaurant?

MP3 04

你最喜歡去哪間餐廳吃飯？

Josh ▸ I love going to the buffet restaurant in Hyatt hotel. They have the best selection of seafood and good range of carvery. Their oyster is absolutely to die for! I don't go there that often because it is quite pricy, probably only for special occasions like my birthday. I think to indulge yourself once a while is pretty reasonable!

喬許 ▸ 我最喜歡去凱悅飯店吃自助餐了！他們的海鮮種類很多樣，爐烤肉塊的選擇也還不少。他們的生蠔超美味的！我是不太常去吃，因為實在還蠻貴的，大部分都是特殊節日像生日之類的才會去。偶而犒賞一下自己也不過分吧！

Abby ▸ Most people might give me a hard time about the choice of food, but my favourite restaurant is actually KFC, I go there at least once a week. I know fast

food is not good for you, but their fried chicken is just so irresistible! I do try to health it up by getting salad instead of chips. It makes me feel less guilty for eating junk food!

艾比 ▸ 大部分的人聽到我最喜歡的餐廳都會皺眉頭，可是我真的很喜歡肯德基，我至少一個星期去一次。我知道速食對身體不好，可是他們的炸雞真的很難抗拒!我會把薯條換成沙拉來均衡一下，這樣我也比較沒有吃垃圾食物的罪惡感。

Cameron ▸ I must tell you about this restaurant called Buddha's hand. Their vegetarian food is top shelf! I go there with my family when we have visitors. My favourite dish is the sweet and sour monk fish. The monk fish is crispy on the outside and soft in the centre. It is amazing! I mean, with food like that, it is actually not so bad being a vegetarian.

卡麥倫 ▸ 我一定要跟你推薦這家叫"佛手"的餐廳，他們的速食真的非常棒! 我家如果有客人來的時候，都會去那裏吃飯。我最喜歡的那道菜是糖醋素魚，素魚炸的外酥內軟，真的很美味。其實如果吃的是這樣的菜色，那吃素真的一點也不痛苦。

Park

公園

台灣其實到處都有公園，一般常見的公園有，中央公園（central park）、濕地公園（wetland park）、親子公園（family park）、河岸公園（riverside park）、森林公園（forest park）、紀念公園（memorial park）、國家公園（national park）等等。大部分公園裡都可以看到兒童遊樂設施（Kid's playgroud）、運動設施（exercise equipment）、人造湖（man-made lake）、草地（lawn）、花叢（meadow）。清晨，傍晚或假日也是公園人最多的時候，在公園可以從事的戶外活動有: 烤肉（BBQ）、溜冰（roller blading ）、跑步（jogging）、散步（going for a walk）、野餐（picnic）、賞鳥（bird watching）、太極拳（Tai-Chi）、看日出（sun rise）等等。

雅思主題字彙表

❶ 中央公園	central park
❷ 濕地公園	wetland park
❸ 親子公園	family park

④ 河岸公園	riverside park
⑤ 森林公園	forest park
⑥ 紀念公園	memorial park
⑦ 國家公園	National park
⑧ 兒童遊樂設施	Kid's playground
⑨ 運動設施	exercise equipment
⑩ 人造湖	man-made lake
⑪ 草地	lawn
⑫ 花叢	meadow
⑬ 烤肉	BBQ
⑭ 溜冰	roller blading
⑮ 跑步	jogging
⑯ 散步	going for a walk
⑰ 野餐	picnic
⑱ 賞鳥	bird watching
⑲ 太極拳	Tai Chi
⑳ 看日出	sun rise

Can you recommend a park for family with young kids?

你可以推薦一個適合有小孩的家庭去的公園嗎？

Josh ▸ I think Kenting National park is great for kids of all ages. There are natural reserves up in the hilly area for kids like bushes and hiking. And if they are into water sports, Kenting National park is right next to the beach. Young kids can have a splash by the beach and older ones can go for snorkelling or surfing if they are adventurous.

喬許 ▸ 我覺得墾丁國家公園最適合小孩了，不管是大小孩還是小小孩。喜歡爬山健走的可以到山丘的自然公園去走走。如果喜歡水上活動的直接到墾丁國家公園的旁的海灘，小小孩可以玩玩水，大一點愛刺激的還可以去浮潛或是衝浪。

Abby ▸ It would have to be the Central park in Kaohsiung. The park is totally designed for kids, there is a playground, a water fountain, and small maze. The best part is the birdlife there. There are lots of pigeons and ducks by the pond. I was lucky I didn't get pooed on! I think family with young kids would really enjoy it.

艾比 ▸ 那一定是高雄的中央公園了！這個公園完全為小孩設計的，有遊樂場，噴水池還有一個小迷宮。最特別的是這裡鳥類很多，池塘附近聚集的很多鴿子還有野鴨，還好沒有鳥在我頭上大便。我覺得有小孩的家庭一定會很喜歡這裡。

Cameron ▸ I would recommend Da-An Forest Park in Taipei. here are slides, swing sets, and a large jungle gym. It is difficult to find a decent park for kids in Taipei because of the value of the land. I am glad at least the kids got a nice park to go to.

卡麥倫 ▸ 我會推薦台北的大安森林公園。有溜滑梯，盪鞦韆還有很大的攀爬設備。在台北因為寸土寸金，所以很難找到適合小孩的公園，還好至少有它們這個地方可以去。

Museum

博物館

博物館總是給人很嚴肅的感覺，但其實博物館有很多不同的類型，例如：美術館（Art museum）、科工館（science and technology museum）、歷史博物館（history museum）、史前文化博物館（prehistory museum）、星象館（astronomy museum）、海洋博物館（marine science and technology museum）。在博物館裡的展示廳（showroom）常常會舉辦不同主題（theme）的展覽（exhibition）或展示（display）。為了讓民眾對展示的主題有更深入的了解，博物館裡也常會有互動體驗區（interaction games），也可以預約導覽員（guide）做解說服務。博物館常常是學校的戶外教學（school excursion）的首選。大部分的博物館需要門票（admission）、成人（adult fare）與小孩的價格不同，另外還有博愛票（concession ticket）或團體折扣（group discount）。

雅思主題字彙表

❶ 美術館	art museum

② 科工館	science and technology museum
③ 歷史博物館	history museum
④ 史前文化博物館	prehistory museum
⑤ 星象館	astronomy museum
⑥ 海洋博物館	marine science and technology museum
⑦ 展示廳	showroom
⑧ 主題	theme
⑨ 展覽	exhibition
⑩ 展示	display
⑪ 互動體驗區	interaction zone
⑫ 導覽員	guide
⑬ 學校的戶外教學	school excursion
⑭ 門票	admission
⑮ 成人票	adult fare
⑯ 博愛票	concession ticket
⑰ 團體折扣	group discount
⑱ 百科全書	wikipedia
⑲ 有娛樂性的	entertaining
⑳ 有知識性的	informative

一問三答

When was the last time you visited a museum?

你上次去博物館是什麼時候?

Josh ▸ Only two weeks ago when my cousins came down to Kenting to visit us. We took them to National museum of Marine Biology & Aquarium in Ping Tong. We had a great time learning about different types of corals and fishes from different parts of Taiwan. I think the place is really well setup. It is both fun and educational.

喬許 ▸ 我兩個禮拜前才去過，我表弟他們來墾丁找我們時，我們帶他們到屏東的海洋生物博物館。我們學到很多跟珊瑚有關的知識，還有台灣海域不同的魚種。我覺得海生館設計得很好，讓人覺得很好玩也很有教育性。

Abby ▸ I think it was a few years ago when I first moved to Taipei. My family and it took a trip to National Palace museum to check out all the treasures that

Chiang Kai Shek allegedly took with him to Taiwan when he lost the war with Chairman Mao. There are some really awesome things there, and my favourite is the piece of jade that looks like a piece of stewed pork.

艾比 ▸ 好像是幾年前我剛搬到台北的時候，我跟我家人到故宮去玩。去看看傳説中國共內戰蔣公撤退台灣時，從大陸運來的寶物。實在有很多稀世珍寶，可是我最喜歡的是一塊看起來像滷肉的玉石。

Cameron ▸ I think the last time would be when I was on a school excursion to the National museum of Nature Science in Taichung. The memory is a bit vague, but I still remember the big dinosaur skeleton in the main entrance, I thought that was so cool when I was a kid!

卡麥倫 ▸ 我想最後一次去應該是國中時到台中科博館戶外教學的時候。我的記憶已經很模糊了，我只記得入口的地方有一個很大的恐龍骨架，我小時候覺得那很酷。

Hotel

飯店

國內外一般常見的飯店有商務旅館（business hotel）、渡假飯店（holiday resort）、膠囊旅館（capsule hotel）、青年旅館（youth hostel）、汽車旅館（Motel）。飯店裡的基本的房型可以分成單人房（single room）、雙人房（double room）、家庭房（family room）、小木屋（villa）。而客人可以依情況要求兩小床（twin-share）。與房客比較有接觸的飯店的員工大概有櫃台人員（receptionist）、門房（porter / concierge）、房間清潔人員（housekeeper），大部分的飯店員工都可以接受小費（tips）。很多房客是從硬體設備優劣來做為選擇飯店的標準，設備方面來說有登記櫃台（check in/check out counter）、大廳（lobby）、溫水泳池（heated pool）、健身房（gym）、蒸氣室（sauna room）等等。

雅思主題字彙表

❶ 商務旅館	business hotel
❷ 渡假飯店	holiday resort
❸ 膠囊旅館	capsule hotel

④ 青年旅館	youth hostel
⑤ 汽車旅館	motel
⑥ 單人房	single room
⑦ 雙人房	double room
⑧ 家庭房	family room
⑨ 小木屋	villa
⑩ 兩小床	twin-share
⑪ 櫃台人員	receptionist
⑫ 門房	porter / concierge
⑬ 房間清潔人員	housekeeper
⑭ 小費	Tips
⑮ 登記櫃台	check in/ check out counter
⑯ 大廳	lobby
⑰ 溫水泳池	heated pool
⑱ 健身房	gym
⑲ 蒸氣室	sauna room
⑳ 客房服務	room service

一問三答

How do you choose a hotel when you are on holiday?

你去度假的時候會選擇住怎樣的旅館?

Josh ▸ I always go for Youth hostel or back packer's hostel if I am on holiday. Normally, they are not far from the hustle and bustle. I am looking for people to party with and the guests there are normally looking for a good time, too! I am not picky about the facility, as long as it is clean and functional.

喬許 ▸ 我度假的時候不是選擇青年旅館就是背包客棧，通常那些旅館都離熱鬧的地方不遠。我也是想要找志同道合的人一起去跑趴玩樂，大部分的住客也都是這種心態。硬體設備如何我是不太介意，只要乾淨能用就好。

Abby ▸ I normally travel on a shoe string budget, so the cheaper the better is what I say. But I don't like to share the room with strangers, so I would look for a small hotel maybe two or three stars. If you look hard enough, there are some really good bargains online if you book early.

艾比 ▸ 我通常預算都很低，所以越便宜越好。可是我又不喜歡跟陌生人同住一室，所以我大概都找一些小的二星或三星飯店。如果你努力一點找，通常網路上都有一些很便宜的早鳥專案。

Cameron ▸ I like to spoil myself a bit when I am on holiday. I worked hard to save the money for the trip, and I just want to reward myself. I like a fancy place preferably with an outdoor pool and breakfast. There is nothing better than waking up to a breakfast buffet.

卡麥倫 ▸ 我度假的時候喜歡享受，畢竟錢是我辛苦工作賺來的，回饋一下自己有什麼不對。如果價格可以接受的話我喜歡高級一點的地方，最好要有室外游泳池還要含早餐。誰不喜歡早上起床就有豐盛的自助早餐吃。

Sport Center

活動中心

活動中心可以是廣義的公共活動中心（community center）租借給私人教授課程（private lessons）例如劍道（kendo）、跆拳道（taekwondo）、空手道（karate）、柔道（judo），有氧舞蹈（aerobic）。另外可以提供運動休息的場所也可以算是活動中心，例如籃球場（basketball court）、羽球場（badminton court）、棒球場（baseball stadium），網球場（tennis court）、足球場（football field）、高爾夫球場（golf driving range）、游泳俱樂部（swimming club）、健身中心（fitness center）、舞蹈教室（dance studio）、瑜珈教室（yoga studio）等等。有的活動中心是採會員制（membership only）、入會的合約上都有明細和規定（terms and conditions），中途若是不想上了很可能也無法全額退費（non-refundable）。

雅思主題字彙表

❶ 公共活動中心	community center
❷ 私人教授課程	private lessons

③ 劍道	kendo
④ 跆拳道	taekwondo
⑤ 空手道	karate
⑥ 柔道	judo
⑦ 有氧舞蹈	aerobic
⑧ 籃球場	basketball court
⑨ 羽球場	badminton court
⑩ 棒球場	baseball stadium
⑪ 網球場	tennis court
⑫ 足球場	football field
⑬ 高爾夫球場俱樂部	golf driving range
⑭ 游泳會	swimming club
⑮ 健身中心	fitness center
⑯ 舞蹈教室	dance studio
⑰ 瑜珈教室	yoga studio
⑱ 會員制	membership only
⑲ 明細和規定	terms and conditions
⑳ 無法全額退費	non-refundable

Do you exercise in a sport center?

你會去活動中心運動嗎？

Josh ▸ No, not really, because the sport center does not really offer things that I like to do. I am more an outdoor person than an indoor person. I like open water swimming and diving which are not something you can do indoors. Nothing beats the smell of the ocean and the wind blowing on my face

喬許 ▸ 沒有，並不會，因為活動中心並沒有我喜歡的運動項目，而且我喜歡自己去。我是一個很愛戶外運動的人，我喜歡到海裡游泳還有潛水，這些都不能在室內進行。我最享受大海的味道還有暖風吹在臉上的感覺了！

Abby ▸ I actually do, I take hip hop dance classes in China Youth Corps Center every Thursday night. The fees are affordable and facility

is quite good, too. The most important thing is, the instructor is really hot, he's got really nice six packs. I love it when he gives me the one on one attention and personally shows me the moves!

艾比 ▸ 其實有，我每個星期四晚上都在救國團的活動中心上嘻哈舞課。學費便宜而且設備也還不錯，最棒的是教練很帥，他的腹肌好性感。我超愛他單獨過來一對一指導教我怎麼跳！

Cameron ▸ Yes, I do. Once every couple of months I will go to the baseball batting cage to practice batting. It is good fun but I can't afford to go every week, it just gets too expensive. Most of the weekend I just practice with my friends in the local school field.

卡麥倫 ▸ 有，我會去。每隔幾個月我就會去棒球打擊練習場練習擊球。是很好玩可是我沒辦法每個星期都去，實在負擔不起。大部分的周末我都是跟朋友在附近的學校操場練習。

Outdoor place

戶外地點

戶外地點可以是觀光景點，例如民俗村（culture village）、主題樂園、鳥園（bird park）、植物園（botanic park）之類或是國家公園（national park）、沙丘（sand dune），或是住家附近的空地或廣場（square），中正紀念堂（Chiang Kai Shek Memorial Hall）、文化中心（culture centre）、動物農場（animal farm）。提了地點之後也要說明為什麼喜歡特定地點的原因，可能對你來說有紀念性（significant），有特殊的風景（scenery），例如吊橋（hanging bridge）、瀑布（waterfall）之類，或是可以從事你喜歡的活動例如可以滑沙（sand boarding）、露營（camping）、採水果（fruit picking）、攀岩（rock climbing）、看夜景（check out the nightscape）、約會或家庭聚會（family gathering）。其實露天夜市也是一個選項，可以享受美食或是喜歡人聲鼎沸（hustle and bustle）的感覺。

雅思主題字彙表

❶ 民俗村	culture village
❷ 鳥園	bird park

③ 植物園	botanic park
④ 國家公園	National park
⑤ 沙丘	sand dune
⑥ 空地或廣場	square
⑦ 中正紀念堂	Chiang Kai Shek Memorial Hall
⑧ 文化中心	Culture Centre
⑨ 有動物的農場	animal farm
⑩ 紀念性	significant
⑪ 風景	scenery
⑫ 吊橋	hanging bridge
⑬ 瀑布	waterfall
⑭ 滑沙	sand boarding
⑮ 露營	camping
⑯ 採水果	fruit picking
⑰ 攀岩	rock climbing
⑱ 看夜景	check out the nightscape
⑲ 家庭聚會	family gathering
⑳ 人聲鼎沸	hustle and bustle

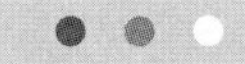

Where is your favourite outdoor place?

你最喜歡的戶外地點是哪裡？

Josh ▸ There are lots of beaches in Kenting, but my favourite spot is the beach called Bai-sha which means white sandy beach in Chinese. It is a secluded area hidden among the palm trees. If you have watched the movie " Life of Pi" you would have seen the beach already, it is where Pi was washed up from the ocean.

喬許 ▸ 墾丁有很多海灘，可是我有個最愛的景點叫白砂，白砂中文的意思就是白色的沙灘。那是一個隱密的地方，被層層的椰子樹圍住。你如果看過電影" 少年 Pi 的奇幻漂流" 那你就知道那個地方長什麼樣子了，就是 Pi 被沖上岸的那個的地點。

Abby ▸ My favourite outdoor place would have been the rooftop of my building. It is like my secret hideout as well. I love to go up there just to chill out and do a

bit of gardening to tidy up my pot plants. It calms me right down.

艾比 ▸ 我最喜歡的戶外景點就是我家的頂樓了！那也是我的私房景點，獨處的地方。如果我很想放鬆的時候我就會上頂樓澆澆花，整理一下盆栽。這使我冷靜下來。

Cameron ▸ I love the hot springs in Bei-Tou, and my favourite outdoor hot spring is in this boutique hotel. Their hot spring area literately hangs off the cliff, and you feel like you are surrounded by mountains when you are in it. I love taking my girlfriend there, it is perfect for couples, the view is unbelievable!

卡麥倫 ▸ 我喜歡北投的溫泉，而且我發現了一個泡溫泉最棒的地點，就是這間精品飯店。它的溫泉區就是真的是懸掛在山邊，在那裡你真的可以感受到群山環繞的感覺。我最喜歡帶我女朋友去那裡，很適合情人去，景色實在太美了！

Neighbor

鄰居

鄰居通常充滿各式各樣不同性格的人，有的鄰居媽媽很外向（outgoing）、愛講話（chatty）、熱心（enthusiastic）、愛嘮叨（nagging），又很八卦。有些則很冷漠（keep things to themselves），文靜（quiet）、低調（low key），自私（selfish），古怪（weird），有潔癖的人（clean freak）就比較沒什麼來往。也有那種很假（pretentious）又愛炫耀（showoff）家裡的財富或是兒女的成就，總是在比較的鄰居。以家庭背景來說，有的可能是問題家庭（dysfunctional family），或是獨居有外傭（maid）照顧的老人、做生意的老闆（bnusiness owner）、小吃攤商（hawker stall vendor）、上班族（office worker）等等，可以針對他們的職業或特性來做形容。

雅思主題字彙表

❶ 外向	outgoing
❷ 愛講話	chatty
❸ 熱心	enthusiastic

④ 愛嘮叨	nagging
⑤ 冷漠	keep things to themselves
⑥ 文靜	quiet
⑦ 低調	low key
⑧ 自私	selfish
⑨ 古怪	weird
⑩ 有潔癖的人	clean freak
⑪ 很假	pretentious
⑫ 愛炫耀	showoff
⑬ 問題家庭	dysfunctional family
⑭ 外傭	maid
⑮ 做生意的老闆	business owner
⑯ 小吃攤商	hawker stall vendor
⑰ 上班族	office worker
⑱ 單親	sin gle parent
⑲ 里長	borough chief
⑳ 社區守望相助義工	neighborhood watch volunteers

一問三答

Q 10 Do you like your neighbors?

MP3 10

你喜歡你的鄰居嗎？

Josh ▸ My neighbors are nice people, but sometimes I really want to avoid them. Most of them are old ladies around my mother's age, they are so gossiping and always trying to play matchmaker. They all tried to set me up with girls when I was single, I am sure if they found out I've got a steady girlfriend, they would hassle me to get married every time they see me.

喬許 ▸ 我的鄰居人都不錯可是有時候我真的想躲她們。她們大部分都是看著我長大的，跟我媽年紀差不多的太太們。她們真的很八卦而且很愛幫人做媒。我單身的時候每個人都想幫我介紹，我如果跟她們說我有女朋友了，她們一定一天到晚催我結婚。

Abby ▸ I don't have much to do with my neighbors because I am always at work, and I have been moving

around a bit since I moved to Taipei. I know they have a couple of young kids and they do get a bit noisy now and again, but there is no drama. I stay up late anyway, so they wouldn't keep me awake.

艾比 ▸ 我跟我鄰居不太熟，因為我大部分時間都在加班，而且我搬到台北之後也常搬家。我知道他們有兩個小孩，有時候會有點吵鬧，可是沒有什麼大問題。反正我也都很晚睡，不會吵到我。

Cameron ▸ Yeah, I get along with my neighbors. Mrs. Huang next door is my favourite because she is forever bringing us stuff. She makes the best rice dumplings. I always look forward to tasting her dumplings for dragon boat festival.

卡麥倫 ▸ 是的，我跟我鄰居們很好。尤其是隔壁的黃媽媽，我最喜歡她了。因為她常常會帶東西給我們，她包的粽子真的超好吃的！我端午節最期待的就是吃她的粽子了。

Teacher
老師

老師給人的印象很多元（diverse），可能很無趣（dull）、古板（conservative）、嚴肅（serious）、看起來很兇（mean-looking）、高高在上（superior）的或是很有熱忱（passionate）、很有活力（active）、可以讓人親近的（approachable），對學生很關愛（caring）、幽默（funny）、很聰明（witty）、很無私的（selfless）、有影響力的（influential）、有説服力的（convincing）。可以從與老師的對話或是他課堂上的小故事，甚至是學校對老師的表揚獲認證（recognition）都可以讓人受到感動及啟發。

雅思主題字彙表

❶ 很多元	diverse
❷ 很無趣	dull
❸ 古板	conservative
❹ 嚴肅	serious
❺ 看起來很兇	mean-looking
❻ 高高在上	superior

⑦ 很有熱忱	passionate
⑧ 很有活力	active
⑨ 可以讓人親近的/親切的	approachable
⑩ 很關愛的	caring
⑪ 幽默	funny
⑫ 很聰明	witty
⑬ 很無私的	selfless
⑭ 有影響力的	influential
⑮ 有說服力的	convincing
⑯ 認證	recognition
⑰ 獎座	award
⑱ 潛力	potential
⑲ 很用心	attentive
⑳ 很為人著想的	considerate

一問三答

Have you ever been inspired by a teacher?

曾經有老師讓你覺得受到他的感動及啟發嗎?

Josh ▸ I was once told by my English teacher that I would never make it through high school because I never handed in any homework. I used to hate her, but when I got older, I am actually quite thankful for what she said because I worked twice as hard just to prove her wrong, and look at me now!

喬許 ▸ 我以前的一個英文老師跟我說我高中應該畢不了業，因為我從來不交功課。我曾經很討厭她，可是等我長大一點之後，我其實還蠻感謝她的，因為我為了證明她是錯的，我真的加倍努力，才有現在的成就。

Abby ▸ Most of the teachers I had just seem to take teaching as a job. I don't think they would go extra miles to encourage students to achieve their potentials, at least not to me. It is a bit unfortunate, I couldn't think of anyone that inspired me.

艾比 ▸ 我遇到的老師大部分都沒什麼熱忱，教書對他們來說好像只是一份薪水而已。我覺得他們不太會特別用心去鼓勵學生，激發他們的潛力，我遇到的都是這樣。也算我運氣不好啦！這樣來說的話，沒有唉，我沒有遇到這樣的老師。

Cameron ▸ Yes, there are a few actually. I consider myself pretty lucky that I was surrounded by teachers with passion and kind words throughout my school life. I always remember when my math teacher pulled me aside and told me I should pursue my studies overseas, that is what I am working towards.

卡麥倫 ▸ 有，其實有好幾個。我覺得我的求學生涯還蠻幸運的，我身邊的老師們都很有熱忱而且都很會講鼓勵人的話。我一直都記得，我的數學老師曾經把我拉到一邊私底下跟我說，我應該出國留學，這也是我一直追求的目標。

Ideal partner

理想情人

理想情人就離不開外在（appearance）和內在條件（inner beauty）了，比如說外表要高大、迷人的（charming）、斯文的（clean shaven）、粗曠的（rugged）、運動型（athletic）、很壯的（masculine）、瘦瘦的（slim）。內在條件例如: 性格（personality） 、體貼（thoughtful）、溫柔（tender）、文靜的（quiet）。還有一些需要相處才會發現的個人習慣，例如意見很多的（opinionated ） 主導/強勢的（dominating）、很有控制慾的（controlling）、聽話的（obedient）。以前的人挑老公會喜歡以家庭為重的（family oriented）、孝順的，可是如果過度的話就變成媽寶（mommy's boy）。還有 家世背景（family background）、學歷背景（education background）都會列入考慮的範圍內。

雅思主題字彙表

❶ 外在條件	appearance
❷ 內在條件	inner beauty
❸ 帥氣的	charming

④ 斯文的	clean shaven
⑤ 粗曠的	rugged
⑥ 運動型	athletic
⑦ 很壯的	masculine
⑧ 瘦瘦的	slim
⑨ 性格	personality
⑩ 體貼	thoughtful
⑪ 溫柔	sweet
⑫ 文靜的	quiet
⑬ 意見很多的	opinionated
⑭ 主導/強勢的	dominating
⑮ 很有控制慾的	controlling
⑯ 聽話的	obedient
⑰ 以家庭為重的	family oriented
⑱ 媽寶	mommy's boy
⑲ 家世背景	family background
⑳ 學歷	education background

一問三答

What do you look for in an ideal partner?

你心中的理想情人應該是怎麼樣的？

Josh ▸ I think my ideal partner would have to love outdoor sports as much as I do because I want to be able to share my passion with her. A hot beach babe would be the type of girl I normally go for, but my mother might not agree with me on that one.

喬許 ▸ 我的理想情人應該要跟我一樣熱愛戶外活動，因為我想要有一個可以分享相同興趣的伴侶。海灘辣妹是我最喜歡的型，可是我媽就不覺得她們適合我。

Abby ▸ I would love to meet a guy who is nice and sweet, tall and handsome with charming eyes. I don't mind his background as long as we can talk to each other and being on the same page about what we want in life. I think Orlando Bloom from Lord of the rings would be the perfect one! I just can't resist a clean shaven guy.

艾比 ▸ 我希望有一天我可以遇到一個溫柔體貼的男孩，最好是高大帥氣還有一雙迷人的眼睛。我不太介意他的背景如何，只要可以溝通，心靈相通，對未來的想法一樣就好。我覺得如果像魔戒中的奧蘭多布魯那就太棒了！我最喜歡斯文型的男生。

Cameron ▸ I thought I would prefer a quiet person like me, but I found I am always attracted to girls who are outgoing and bubbly, I guess it is just to make up for my shortcoming. Maybe someone from a similar educational background, so we will have something in common to talk about.

卡麥倫 ▸ 我以為我自己會喜歡跟我類似的人，可是我發現我卻覺得外向活潑的女生很吸引人，應該是跟我互補吧。如果跟我有類似的教育背景的話我們就會更有話說。

Friend

朋友

形容朋友可以從外表，與他有關的特殊事件或他的性格和行為下手。外表，如:髮型（hairdo）、身高（height）、體型（body shape），或是臉上或身上的特徵（unique feature），例如痣（mole）、雙眼皮（double eyelid）、鼻環（nose piercing）、刺青（tattoo）。也可以從你們的友誼來說起，例如願意支持你的（supportive）、心靈相通（see eye to eye）、分不開的（inseparable）、不計較（forgiving）、興趣相同（share common interests）、一起玩（hang out）、很合得來（get along）。

雅思主題字彙表

❶ 髮型	hairdo
❷ 身高	height
❸ 體型	body shape
❹ 特徵	unique feature
❺ 痣	mole
❻ 雙眼皮	double eyelid

⑦ 穿鼻環	nose piercing
⑧ 刺青	tattoo
⑨ 願意支持你的	supportive
⑩ 心靈相通	see eye to eye
⑪ 分不開的/如膠似漆	inseparable
⑫ 不計較	forgiving
⑬ 興趣相同	share common interests
⑭ 一起玩	hang out
⑮ 很合得來	get along
⑯ 很關心人	caring
⑰ 可以信任的	trustworthy
⑱ 讓人很舒服的	comforting
⑲ 真心的/不虛偽的	genuine
⑳ 站在你這邊	on your side

Q 13 Please describe a close friend.

MP3 13

請形容你的一個好朋友

Josh ▸ It would have to be my buddy Dylan. I grow up with Dylan because he is my next door neighbor, he is like the brother I never had. We both love outdoor sports. I talk to him about everything, and he knows all my secrets!

喬許 ▸ 我想說我的麻吉狄倫，我跟狄倫從小一起長大，他是我的隔壁鄰居，我一直把他當親兄弟看。我們兩個都喜歡戶外活動，也都一直念同一所學校。我跟他無話不談，我的秘密他都知道。

Abby ▸ Tina is a friend of mine, I met her at the Hip hop class. She also really enjoys dancing. We hang out a lot on the weekend because she also doesn't have a boyfriend. I did not realize she actually knows my brother until I added her as a friend on Facebook. What a small world.

艾比 ▸ 我有一個朋友叫婷娜，我在嘻哈舞課認識她的，她也很喜歡跳舞。我們週末常常一起出去，因為她也沒有男朋友。我加她臉書好友的時候才發現原來她認識我哥。這世界真小。

Cameron ▸ My best friend from high school is called Ah-Hsiung. We love to play basketball together. He is tall and skinny like a stick, but his build is perfect for basketball. All the juniors go crazy for him when he is playing. He was so popular when we were in high school, and he still is now with the ladies.

卡麥倫 ▸ 我高中的好朋友叫阿雄，我們很愛一起打籃球。他又高又瘦像根竹竿一樣，可是這種身型很適合打籃球。只要他一上場全部的學妹都會為他加油，他高中時代很受歡迎，他現在還是很受女生的青睞。

Child

小孩

除了鄰居的小孩，常接觸的小孩應該就是表弟表妹（cousins）或是姪子（nephew） 姪女（niece）了。大部分的小孩天生就是天真無邪（innocent）、活潑好動（full of beans）、調皮（naughty）、有想像力的（good imagination）、有創造力的（creative）。但也不是每個小孩都沒有煩惱，小孩可能面臨過動（hyperactive）、過胖（overweight）、或是不停地上補習班（cram school）的問題。在台灣小孩如果不是祖父母幫忙帶，就是送幼稚園（kindergarten），在幼稚園裡常做的活動除了唱歌跳舞之外，還有拼圖（puzzle）、勞作（Arts and crafts）、做早操（morning exercises）等等。

雅思主題字彙表

❶ 表弟、表妹	cousins
❷ 姪子	nephew
❸ 姪女	niece
❹ 天真無邪	innocent

⑤ 活潑好動	full of beans
⑥ 調皮	naughty
⑦ 有想像力的	good imagination
⑧ 有創造力的	creative
⑨ 過動	hyperactive
⑩ 過胖	overweight
⑪ 補習班	cram school
⑫ 幼稚園	kindergarten
⑬ 拼圖	puzzle
⑭ 勞作	arts and crafts
⑮ 做早操	morning exercises
⑯ 才藝班	talent class
⑰ 接送	pick up and drop off
⑱ 保母	nanny
⑲ 托兒所	childcare
⑳ 照顧小孩	babysitting

MP3 14

Do you like children?

你喜歡小孩嗎?

Josh ▸ I love kids, especially my five-year-old nephew – Jordon. Jordon is great. He loves surfing as much as I do. He is very talented. I always take him to the beach on Sundays and teach him how to surf. I can't wait for him to grow up and be my surf buddy!

喬許 ▸ 我超愛小孩的，尤其是我五歲的外甥喬丹。喬丹很棒，他跟我一樣愛衝浪，他也很有天分，我每個星期天都帶他到海邊教他衝浪。我好期待他趕快長大，可以當我的衝浪夥伴!

Abby ▸ Yes, I do. I am very close to my nieces; I volunteer to pick them up from school everyday because my sister couldn't get off work in time. I really enjoy spending time with them. They get excited about the simplest thing. It is such a pleasure to see the smile on their faces.

艾比 ▸ 嗯，我喜歡。我跟我的姪女們很好，因為我姊來不及下班去接他們，我都自願去接。我很喜歡跟他們在一起，他們可以因為很沒什麼的事情就很高興，我很喜歡看他們的笑臉！

Cameron ▸ Honestly, I am a bit scared of kids actually because I don't know what to say to them. and every time I try to play with them, they just end up in tears. I tried very hard to be a popular uncle but no matter what I do, it just wouldn't work.

卡麥倫 ▸ 說真的，我其實有一點怕小孩，因為我不知道要跟他們說什麼。每次我過去跟他們玩，都會把他們弄哭。我也很想當個受歡迎的叔叔，可是就沒辦法。

Animal

動物

動物可以分不同的種類（species）或品種（breed）。在台灣不容易見到大型的野生動物（wild animal），卻有不少瀕臨絕種的動物（endangered animal）。一般人接觸最多的動物除了流浪動物之外，大概就就是家庭裡的寵物（pets）了。一般台灣人的家都沒有前後院，養寵物常常是缺點（disadvantage）大於優點（advantage），因為沒有足夠的空間，動物養在客廳或浴室是常有的事。 要是寵物的性格溫馴（tame）、膽小（timid） 那倒是無所謂，如果遇到兇猛（ferocious）、不受控制的（feral）的動物，就很可能被棄養（being abandoned） 。一直以來與動物相關的活動就很受歡迎，例如看野生動物旅行（safari）、餵食秀（feeding show）。流浪動物領養（adoption）的概念也越來越普遍，所領養的動物都需要晶片植入（chip implantation）。

雅思主題字彙表

❶ 種類	species
❷ 品種	breed

③ 野生動物	wild animal
④ 瀕臨絕種的動物	endangered animal
⑤ 家庭裡的寵物	pets
⑥ 缺點	disadvantage
⑦ 優點	advantage
⑧ 溫馴	tame
⑨ 兇猛	ferocious
⑩ 膽小	timid
⑪ 不受控制的	feral
⑫ 被棄養	being abandoned
⑬ 看野生動物旅行	safari
⑭ 領養	adoption
⑮ 餵食秀	feeding show
⑯ 晶片植入	chip implantation
⑰ 動物遷徙	animal migration
⑱ 夜行性	nocturnal
⑲ 哺乳類	mammals
⑳ 爬蟲類	reptile

Q 15 What is your favorite animal?

你喜歡什麼動物?

Josh ▸ I would love to have a pet chameleon; I think it would be really cool! They look kind of scary, and people often think chameleons are ferocious, but they are actually quite tame. They don't really bite unless they are agitated. They eat with their tongue just like frogs. I don't own one because they are just too hard to look after.

喬許 ▸ 我很想要有一隻變色龍，我覺得它很酷！他們的外型有點嚇人，讓很多人覺得變色龍很兇猛，其實他們很溫馴。除非他們被激怒了，不然不會咬人。他們跟青蛙一樣用舌頭吃昆蟲。我並沒有真的去養因為他們蠻難照顧的。

Abby ▸ Zebra would be my favorite animal, I like the black and white stripes on them. Every time I see one I always try to figure out whether it is a white zebra

with black stripes or a black zebra with white stripes. I was told a herd zebra is called a dazzle because their pattern would actually dazzle the predators' eyes when they gather in large numbers.

艾比 ▸ 我最喜歡的動物是斑馬，我喜歡他們身上的條紋。每一次我看到斑馬我都會仔細的看他到底是有黑條紋的白馬還是有白條紋的黑馬。有人跟我說一群斑馬是用 Dazzle 這個字來形容，原因是他們一大群聚集在一起的時候，身上的條紋會讓掠食者眼撩亂。

Cameron ▸ I love dogs. I think dogs are not only human's best friend. They are also very useful with their excellent sense of smell. Labradors are calm and friendly. They are used as guide dogs. Beagles are used in the airport to detect drugs and prohibited items. I have a lot of respect for dogs.

卡麥倫 ▸ 我喜歡狗，我覺得狗不但是人類最好的朋友，他們靈敏的嗅覺對人類的貢獻很多。就像拉不拉多既穩重又友善，他們可以當導盲犬。米格魯在機場用來偵測毒品還有違禁品。我對狗這種動物很感恩的!

Relatives

親戚

所謂親戚就是大家有共同的祖先（ancestors），比較少見的稱謂（title）有曾祖父母（great grandparents）、舅公叔公（freat uncle）、姨婆（freat auntie）、繼父繼母（step father/mother）等等。親戚不免會有意見不合（disagreement）的爭執（argument）、對立（conflict）。有可能是因為遺囑（will）上遺產繼承（inheritance）、土地分配（land division）的問題。遠房親戚（distant relatives）可能很少見面，見面的機會可能是因為訂婚（engagement）、結婚（tight the knot），喪事（funeral）或是健康問題（health concerns）。

雅思主題字彙表

❶ 祖先	ancestors
❷ 稱謂	title
❸ 曾祖父母	great Grandparents
❹ 舅公叔公	great uncle
❺ 姨婆	great auntie

❻ 繼父繼母	step Father/Mother
❼ 意見不合	disagreement
❽ 爭執	argument
❾ 對立	conflict
❿ 遺囑	will
⓫ 遺產繼承	inheritance
⓬ 土地分配	land division
⓭ 遠房親戚	distant relatives
⓮ 訂婚	engagement
⓯ 結婚/定下來	tight the knot
⓰ 喪事	funeral
⓱ 健康問題	health concerns
⓲ 住院治療	hospitalise
⓳ 加護病房	ICU – Intensive Care Unit
⓴ 再婚	remarried

Do you stay in touch with your relatives?

你跟你的親戚們會保持聯絡嗎？

Josh ▸ It is hard not to stay in touch with your relatives especially when you are from a small town like Heng Chuan. Most of my relatives are my neighbors, and I go to school with some of my cousins, too. I couldn't get away from them even if I wanted to!

喬許 ▸ 不跟親戚聯絡實在太難了，尤其是像我住在恆春這種小鎮。我大部分的親戚都住在附近，我跟我的表兄弟也上同一間學校。就算我不想跟他們聯絡也是會遇到。

Abby ▸ Not really. I personally don't really make any effort to stay in touch with my relatives. It is more my mum's job. She would be the one that calls everyone up during Chinese New Year to say hello, but sometimes you can't even find them. One of my uncles borrowed lots of money from my dad then he run off. There is no way to contact him anyway.

艾比 ▸ 不太會，我個人是不會主動跟我的親戚聯絡，那都是我媽的事。她過年都會跟他們打個電話問好，可是有時候還找不到人呢！就像我一個叔叔跟我爸借了錢就跑路了，根本就找不到人。

Cameron ▸ I am quite close to my cousins because we are all about the same age, although they live in Chia-yi still, there is Skype and LINE. I talk to them quite often.

卡麥倫 ▸ 我跟我的表兄弟們很好因為我們的年紀很接近，雖然他們還住在嘉義。可是現在有 Skype 還有 LINE 很方便，我們常常聯絡。

事件 Weather/Season 天氣/季節

春夏秋冬四季天氣的特性不同，所以可以從適合當季的活動說起。例如，春天可以去看櫻花（cherry blossom），冬天可以去拔蘿蔔（radish harvesting）。或是反過來說某季節的特性對某些活動有限制性（limitation），例如春秋兩季是過敏（allergy）的好發季，所以常需要使用抗過敏的吸入器（inhaler）。或是雨季潮濕，導致家裡的衣物家具常發霉（moldy），所以需要使用除濕機（dehumifier），而雨鞋（gumboots）雨衣（rain coat）不離手。冬季乾冷需要擦乳液（moisturizer）來保濕，出門需要手套（gloves）、圍巾（scarf）。在家的話，暖氣機（heater）、電熱毯（electric blanket）也是必備。若以吃的方面下手，討論每個季節可以享受的季節食材（seasonal ingredient）。

雅思主題字彙表

❶ 賞櫻	cherry blossom
❷ 拔蘿蔔	radish harvesting
❸ 限制性	limitation

④ 季節食材	seasonal ingredient
⑤ 保濕乳液	moisturizer
⑥ 過敏	allergy
⑦ 抗過敏藥物吸入器	inhaler
⑧ 雨季	rainy season
⑨ 發霉	moldy
⑩ 除濕機	dehumidifier
⑪ 雨鞋	gumboots
⑫ 雨衣	rain coat
⑬ 暖氣機	heater
⑭ 電毯	electric blanket
⑮ 圍巾	scarf
⑯ 手套	gloves
⑰ 保溫杯	thermal cup
⑱ 防曬乳	sunscreen
⑲ 曬傷	sun burn
⑳ 汗流浹背	sweaty

一問三答

What do you like to do in your favorite season?

在你最喜歡的季節裡你最喜歡做什麼事?

Josh ▸ I love Summer; I think my skin tone says it all! I love spending time under the sun to build a nice tan. Trust me, the ladies love it! I always volunteer to do the beach watch in Summer because I get to look cool in my board shorts and show off my muscles!

喬許 ▸ 我最愛夏天，看我的膚色也知道。我喜歡在戶外曬太陽，曬成古銅色。相信我，女生都很吃這套! 我夏天常常自願到海邊去當救生員，因為我可以正大光明的穿著我的海灘褲秀肌肉!

Abby ▸ My favorite season is Autumn because it is the best season to enjoy crabs. My favorite thing to do is to go to a seafood restaurant with my family and order seasonal made-to-order stream crabs. We will pay more to order the female crabs because the crab roe is just to die for!

艾比 ▸ 我最喜歡的季節是秋天，因為秋天的螃蟹最肥美！我最喜歡做的事就是跟我家人到海鮮餐廳去點季節限定現點現做的清蒸秋蟹。我們情願付多一點錢要母蟹，因為蟹黃蟹膏真是太美味了！

Cameron ▸ I love Winter, and I love going to the hot spring then because it is just so comforting. Hot springs are very good for your health. The proper way to do it is to soak in the hot spring first then jump into the cold one for a brief moment. Repeat that a few times, it really clears your head.

卡麥倫 ▸ 我最愛冬天了，而且我喜歡冬天去泡溫泉因為真的很療癒。其實泡溫泉對身體很好，泡溫泉正確的方式是先泡溫泉，然後簡短地泡一下冷泉，這樣重複幾次，真的讓人神清氣爽。

School days

求學生涯

一般大家比較熟悉的國小國中科目大概有：國語（mandarin）、數學（mathematic）、英文、物理（physics）、化學（chemistry）、科學（science）、生物（biology）、法律（law）、地理（geography）、歷史（history）、體育（PE-Physical education）、美術（Art）、音樂（music）、電腦（computing）、地球科學（earth science）。喜歡的課程的理由很可能是因為老師的教法或是老師本身的個人魅力，或是課程（curriculum） 的內容（content），還是本身領悟性較強，有天份（gifted）等等。

雅思主題字彙表

❶ 國語	mandarin
❷ 數學	mathematic
❸ 物理	physics
❹ 化學	chemistry
❺ 科學	science
❻ 生物	biology

⑦ 法律	law
⑧ 地理	geography
⑨ 歷史	history
⑩ 體育	PE-Physical Education
⑪ 美術	Art
⑫ 音樂	music
⑬ 電腦	computing
⑭ 地球科學	earth science
⑮ 課程	curriculum
⑯ 內容	content
⑰ 天分	gifted
⑱ 分組作業	group assignment
⑲ 測驗	quiz
⑳ 成績	result
㉑ 技法	technique

What was your favorite subject in your school days?

你求學過程中最喜歡的科目是什麼？

Josh ▸ My favorite subject is biology. I really enjoy learning about animals, insects, and the structure of the human body. My favorite part of the class is the lab work where you get to dissect a frog to see how the muscles work. I still recall some of the girls in my class got so scared of the muscle reflex.

喬許 ▸ 我最喜歡的科目是生物，我很喜歡學跟動物、昆蟲還有人體構造有關的。課堂上我最喜歡的部分是到實驗室去解剖青蛙看肌肉的運作方式。我還記得我們班上的一些女生被肌肉的反射嚇得半死。

Abby ▸ I love Geography the most. My Geography teacher from junior high school was really funny. He made Geography really interesting. He would get us to pretend we were planning a trip to a certain area or country, and I actually learnt a lot from the class. What a brilliant way of teaching!

艾比 ▸ 我最愛上地理課了，我國中的地理老師是個很有趣的人，他讓地理變得很有趣。他會叫我們搜集要到某個地區或是國家玩的資料，我在課堂上學了很多，這種教法真的太聰明了！

Cameron ▸ I really like Art classes because I get to do what I like to do. Preparing for the university entry exam was a stressful time. I always look forward to Art class, so I can take my mind off things. However, Art class in high school doesn't really teach you much technique.

卡麥倫 ▸ 我真的很喜歡美術課，因為我可以做我喜歡的事。準備大學聯考是壓力很大的，只要到美術課我就很高興，因為我可以暫時不用想讀書的事。可是高中的美術課並不會教你什麼畫圖的技法。

Talent

才藝

才藝通常大家會聯想到比較藝術性質的（artistic），例如：鋼琴（piano）、小提琴（violin）、口琴（garmonica）、長笛（flute）、吉他（guitar）、聲樂（vocal）、豎琴（harp）、古箏（chinese zither）、芭蕾舞（ballet）、爵士鼓（drums）、拉丁舞（latino dance）、國標舞（ballroom dancing）、現代舞（modern dance）、油畫（oil painting）、水彩畫（water color painting）。學才藝常會有發表會（concert）比賽之類的活動，當然也會有獎狀（merit certificate）、獎牌（medal）等等。可是相對的學才藝的學費（tuition）還有交通費可是很可觀的。

雅思主題字彙表

❶ 藝術性質的	artistic
❷ 鋼琴	piano
❸ 小提琴	violin
❹ 口琴	harmonica
❺ 長笛	flute

⑥ 吉他	guitar
⑦ 聲樂	vocal
⑧ 豎琴	harp
⑨ 古箏	chinese zither
⑩ 芭蕾舞	ballet
⑪ 爵士鼓	drums
⑫ 拉丁舞	latino dance
⑬ 國標舞	ballroom dancing
⑭ 現代舞	modern dance
⑮ 油畫	oil painting
⑯ 水彩畫	water color painting
⑰ 發表會	concert
⑱ 獎狀	merit Certificate
⑲ 獎牌	medal
⑳ 學費	tuition

一問三答

Q 19 Have you ever taken any talent class

MP3 19

你曾經學過什麼才藝嗎?

Josh ▸ I actually took some Latino dance classes when I was little. I was getting pretty good at it. My speciality is the Cha Cha Cha. I didn't want to continue because I was worried about being judged by my friends. You know how 8 years old boys are like!

喬許 ▸ 其實我小時候學過拉丁舞。我的恰恰還真的跳得不錯。可是我沒有再繼續學下去因為我怕被我的朋友們笑，你知道八歲的小男生就是這樣啊。

Abby ▸ I did Karate when I was in elementary school. I didn't want to do it, but my father wants me to be able to defend myself from the bullies, and he is a firm believer in martial arts. I went along with it for a few years, but I was never any good.

艾比 ▸ 我國小的時候學過跆拳道，我不想學，可是我爸說我一定要學會保護自己，不要被霸凌。他對武術這方面是深信不疑，我順著他的意學了幾年，可是沒學到什麼。

Cameron ▸ I started to learn how to do proper oil painting since I was 10 years old. I have always been artistic and gifted in painting when I was little. My parents have been very supportive, and they decided to enrol me into the oil painting class although I was the youngest student among them.

卡麥倫 ▸ 我從十歲就開始正式的學油畫，我一直都是比較有藝術細胞的，對畫畫這方面很有天賦。我父母親一直都很支持我，所以他們決定送我去油畫班，而我是全班最小的學生。

Driving

開車

開車首先要有駕照（driver's license），台灣考駕照的法定年齡（legal age）是十八歲；而大部分的人都會去駕訓班（driving School）學車，請教練（driving instructor）指導，再到監理所（Road and Traffic Authority）考照，除了筆試之外還要路考（road test）。各國的交通規則（road rules）不盡相同，換國際駕照（international driving permit）時要特別注意。如果出車禍，一般車險（car insurance）都會有理賠（payout），車險的保費（insurance premium）也會因為申請理賠的紀錄而調整（adjust）。有的險種需要繳較高的自付額（out of packet expense），在國外如果要救護車（ambulance）服務也需要保險，否則自費金額很高。

雅思主題字彙表

❶ 駕照	driver's license
❷ 法定年齡	legal age
❸ 駕訓班	driving School

④ 駕訓班老師	driving instructor
⑤ 路考	road test
⑥ 監理所	Road and Traffic Authority
⑦ 交通規則	road rules
⑧ 國際駕照	international driving permit
⑨ 車險	car insurance
⑩ 理賠	payout
⑪ 保費	insurance premium
⑫ 調整	adjust
⑬ 自付額	out of pocket expense
⑭ 救護車	ambulance
⑮ 分隔島	Refuge island
⑯ 超速	Speeding
⑰ 繞道	Detour
⑱ 停車場	Parking lot
⑲ 罰款	Fine
⑳ 傷亡	Casualty

Do you prefer driving or walking?

你喜歡開車還是走路?

Josh ▸ I think it depends on where I am going. If I am only going to the corner 7-11 to get some beer, I much prefer walking to driving since you don't have to worry about parking. The journey is too short for a car ride.

喬許 ▸ 那要看我要去哪裡，如果我只是要去轉角的 7-11 買啤酒那我走路就好了，因為我也不用擔心停車的問題，路程這麼短，根本不需要開車。

Abby ▸ I actually don't own a driver's license which leaves me with no options other than walking or taking public transport everywhere. You wouldn't want to drive in Taipei anyway. Parking is a pain in the ass to find and even if you do find one, it will cost you an arm and a leg.

艾比 ▸ 其實我連駕照都沒有，所以也沒得選擇，不是走路就是坐大眾交通工具。在台北你也不會想開車的，車位難找的要死，就算找到了也是貴得很。

Cameron ▸ I prefer driving for sure, because I need to visit my clients regularly at the industrial park outside of the city. I don't know any other way to get there other than driving! I know finding a place to park the car is a potential problem, but being puncturnal is my priority. There is no other way.

卡麥倫 ▸ 我一定選擇開車，因為我常常需要到近郊的工業區去拜訪客戶。如果不開車我還真不知道我能怎麼去。我知道找車位可能很難找，但是我不準時不行，也只能開車了。

Birthday

生日

生日的慶祝方式，可以辦舞會慶祝，三五好友聚餐（gathering），或是跟家人切蛋糕，或是在公司跟同事慶祝，還有些人根本忙忘了。生日派對需要的物品有蛋糕、外燴（catering）、酒會點心（canapé）、汽水（soft drink）、酒類（alcoholic beverage）和調酒（cocktail）。慶祝生日的方式：驚喜派對（surprise party）、聚餐、整人/惡作劇（prank）、去夜店（go clubbing）、到海邊看日出（watch sunrise）。生日禮物（birthday present）當然也是必備，很多人乾脆直接送禮券（gift voucher），避免買了不合對方心意，還要換貨（exchange）或退貨（return）。

雅思主題字彙表

❶ 聚餐	gathering
❷ 外燴	catering
❸ 酒會點心	canapé
❹ 汽水	soft drink
❺ 酒類	alcoholic beverage

⑥ 烈酒	spirits
⑦ 調酒	cocktail
⑧ 驚喜派對	surprise party
⑨ 整人/惡作劇	prank
⑩ 去夜店	go clubbing
⑪ 看日出	watch sunrise
⑫ 生日禮物	birthday present
⑬ 禮券	gift voucher
⑭ 退貨	return
⑮ 換貨	exchange
⑯ 預購/下次提貨	raincheck
⑰ 邀請函	invitation
⑱ 場地	venue
⑲ 訂位	reservation
⑳ 裝飾/佈置	decoration

一問三答

What do you normally do for your birthday?

你通常都怎麼慶祝生日?

Josh ▸ My birthday is a big thing. My friends like to make big deal out of it. We will normally go somewhere for dinner before heading to the clubs. By the end of the night, we will be so wasted and can't even recall what we did and where we went! But it is always a night to remember.

喬許 ▸ 我的生日是件大事，我的朋友們很喜歡高調慶祝。我們通常會先去吃飯，然後再到酒吧去，我們會盡情狂飲，到最後都不知道我們到底做過什麼去過哪裡，而且絕對是不醉不歸!

Abby ▸ Normally, I will bring a cake to work to share with my coworkers because we get along really well. My boss doesn't normally get in until lunch time, so we are free to do what we want in the office. Some of us might go out for dinner after work, but that's about it.

艾比 ▸ 我通常會帶個蛋糕到公司跟同事一起慶生，因為我跟他們很好。而且我老闆通常午餐時間才會進公司，所以我們蠻自由的。下班後可能跟幾個同事一起吃飯，但大概就是這樣了。

Cameron ▸ My mother is pretty traditional when it comes to my birthday; she insists to make me the pig knuckle noodle soup every year although she knows most likely I would have made dinner plans with my girlfriend to celebrate. However, I would always finish the noodle soup before I go out because I don't want to make her feel bad.

卡麥倫 ▸ 說到我的生日我媽是蠻傳統的，她總是堅持要煮豬腳麵線給我吃，雖然她知道我應該已經跟女朋友約了要出去吃飯慶生。我一定會先吃完她煮的麵線再出去，但那也是她老人家一番心意。

Accident

意外

台灣也因為健保的不周全，所以大部分的人都有私人健康保險（private health insurance）。壽險（life insurance）、意外險（accident insurance）、車險也是非常普遍。如果發生交通意外發生時，可能需要報警留下報案紀錄（police report）以便日後保險公司做定奪。意外發生時，最忌諱慌張（panic），一定要保持冷靜（calm）。如果有人受傷需要送急診（emergency），在救護人員（paramedic）抵達之前也切記不要隨便移動傷患，就怕導致骨折（fracture）或是內出血（internal bleeding）的問題更加嚴重，可能需要及時手術（operation）處理。政府也一直在提倡捐血救人（blood donation），器官捐贈（organ donation）及器官移植（organ transplant）的觀念，一般民眾也越來越能接受。

雅思主題字彙表

❶ 私人健康保險	private health insurance
❷ 壽險	life insurance

③ 意外險	accident insurance
④ 報案紀錄	police report
⑤ 慌張	panic
⑥ 冷靜	calm
⑦ 急診	emergency
⑧ 救護人員	paramedic
⑨ 骨折	fracture
⑩ 內出血	internal bleeding
⑪ 手術	operation
⑫ 捐血救人	blood donation
⑬ 器官捐贈	organ donation
⑭ 器官移植	organ transplant
⑮ 第三人責任險	third party insurance
⑯ 板金	penal
⑰ 保險桿	bumper
⑱ 擋風玻璃	windshield
⑲ 後車箱	boot
⑳ 方向燈	indicator

一問三答

What would you do if you got into a car accident?

你不小心出車禍時會怎麼處理？

Josh ▸ I will first check whether it is my fault or his negligence and whether we need an ambulance or not. If it is just a small bump or a scratch, I will just negotiate with the person and sort it out there and then. It gets too complicated when you get the police involved.

喬許 ▸ 我首先會判斷是我的錯還是對方的失誤，看看我們需不需要救護車。如果只是小擦撞，那我就會跟對方商議是不是能在現場賠償解決就好，叫警察來實在太麻煩了！

Abby ▸ I would totally freak out! I don't have a driver's licence, so I think if I did get into an accident I would be the victim. I guess there is not much I can do, if I got hit by a car, I just hope someone will call the police and the ambulance for me!

艾比 ▸ 我真的會完全嚇壞，我沒有駕照所以我想如果我出了車禍，那我一定是被撞的那個人。我猜如果我被撞了，那我也沒有辦法做什麼事，可能要靠好心人來幫我報警還有叫救護車了。

Cameron ▸ I will call the police for sure because I need the police report to show my insurance agent. I have full coverage for the car and third party insurance. I think I am pretty much covered! I just hope I don't accidently kill someone, then it would be a real nightmare.

卡麥倫 ▸ 我一定會馬上報警，因為我需要給保險公司看報案紀錄。我的車有保全險，而且還有第三人保險，我覺得我沒什麼好擔心的。我只希望我不要意外撞死人就好，那就糟糕了。

Work/study

工作 / 求學

如果被問到工作，可以從職稱（job title）開始做介紹（introduction），可以簡單的陳述工作內容（job description），公司的規模還有公司的結構（company structure）等等。再來可以講講工作的甘苦談，例如老闆不好，一天到晚要工作加班（overtime）、待命（on call），沒有加薪（pay rise）、升職（promotion），沒有績效獎金（commission）、年終紅利（bonus），壓力大（stressful）都可以談。如果是求學的話可以說明目前是哪間學校、幾年級、簡單介紹你的學歷例如主修或擅長的科目。也可以介紹擅長的課外活動及畢業後的展望。

雅思主題字彙表

❶ 職稱	job title
❷ 介紹	introduction
❸ 工作內容	job description
❹ 學士學位	bachelor degree
❺ 碩士學位	master degree
❻ 博士學位	PhD – Doctor of Philosophy

⑦ 成績單	transcript
⑧ 大學畢業證書	testamur
⑨ 錄取標準	entry requirement
⑩ 認證	authenticate
⑪ 待命	on call
⑫ 加班	overtime
⑬ 壓力大	stressful
⑭ 薪水	salary
⑮ 升職	promotion
⑯ 樣品	sample
⑰ 業績	sales target
⑱ 業績獎金	commission
⑲ 年終紅利	yearly bonus
⑳ 待業中	between jobs

一問三答

MP3 23

What do you do?

你目前是做什麼的？

Josh ▸ I graduated from university last year with a bachelor's degree in Physical training. At the moment, I am in the process of getting my application together for the master's degree in Sport Science in the University of Sydney. I hope they will offer a place to me, I can't wait to go surfing in the world famous Bondi beach!

喬許 ▸ 我去年由體育系畢業，目前我正在準備申請雪梨大學運動科學的碩士學位。希望他們會收我，我迫不及待地想去世界出名的邦代海灘衝浪！

Abby ▸ I am a procurement representative in this trading company called "CandyCan ". "CandyCan" specializes in importation of European sweets and confectionary. The best thing of being in this industry is that you're getting the sample for free. I literally get endless supply of the finest Belgium Chocolates.

艾比 ▸ 我是一家叫糖罐子的貿易公司的採購專員，糖罐子是專門進口歐洲的糖果糕餅。做這份工作最好的地方就是廠商會寄樣品給我，我常常收到比利時的高級巧克力呢！

Cameron ▸ I am a sales engineer in a company called Sinclair. Sinclair is a production line machine supplier. My job is to look after my clients and provide them with the technical support and parts. The most annoying thing about my job is that I have to be available on the weekends, too.

卡麥倫 ▸ 我是辛克萊爾的銷售工程師，辛克萊爾是生產線機器的供應商。我的工作是照顧我的客戶，提供技術支援還有零件供應。這份工作最討厭的地方就是我週末也要待命。

Travel

旅遊

旅遊不只是出國旅行，國內當天來回，兩天一夜的微旅行也算。現在因為廉價航空（budget airline）的普遍，出國自助旅行（self-guided tour）的人數眾多。訂房網站 ，訂票網站盛行，訂房訂票需要填寫基本的個人資料（personal detail），須以信用卡（credit card）付款。修改（amendment）日期或取消（cancellation）需要收取手續費（administration fees），有些則無法取消。廉價航空的票價通常只含手提行李（carry-on luggage），機艙行李（check-in luggage）則需要另外付費，乘客也需付費選擇靠走道（aisle seat）或是靠窗（window seat）的位置，餐點（meal）也不包含在內。出國記得確認違禁品（prohibited items）的項目，表格上要確實申報（declare）以免受罰。

雅思主題字彙表

❶ 廉價航空	budget airline
❷ 自助旅行	self-guided tour
❸ 基本的個人資料	personal detail

④ 信用卡	credit card
⑤ 修改	amendment
⑥ 取消	cancellation
⑦ 手續費	administration Fees
⑧ 餐點	meal
⑨ 手提行李	carry-on luggage
⑩ 機艙行李	check-in luggage
⑪ 超重費	overweight fees
⑫ 違禁品	prohibited items
⑬ 報關/申報	declare
⑭ 旅客退稅櫃台	tourist tax refund counter
⑮ 靠走道的座位	aisle seat
⑯ 靠窗的座位	window Seat
⑰ 機艙最前排較寬的座位	bulkhead
⑱ 飛機上準備餐點的廚房區	galley
⑲ 過境旅館	transit hotel
⑳ 轉機櫃檯	transit counter

Q 24 Do you travel a lot?

你常去旅行嗎？

Josh ▸ I did fair a bit of travel in Taiwan with my classmates I have been to most of the famous tourist attractions in Taiwan. The most memorable trip was my surfing competition in Tai-Tung last year. I was so close to winning a prize.

喬許 ▸ 我以前常跟我的同學在台灣到處跑，台灣大大小小的旅遊勝地我大概都去過，可是記憶最深刻的還是我到台東參加衝浪比賽那一次，我差一點就有獎可以拿。

Abby ▸ I don't often go on big trips because it is hard to take time off work. I do like to go overseas, and I have been to Japan and Korea. Sometimes I will go out of my way to visit a place recommended by travel books. But I found most of the time, those places are not as good as how it is described in the book.

艾比 ▸ 我不太常有機會去很久，因為我的工作很難請假。我是蠻喜歡出國的，我去過日本跟韓國。有時候我會特別去旅遊書上介紹過的地方看看，可是我發現那些地方實在沒有書上說的那麼好。

Cameron ▸ Other than going to the hot springs in Yang-Ming mountain, I don't think I travel a lot. I do prefer to hang around the city. Maybe I will go to a different part of the town and try a new café or a new restaurant. That is probably as adventurous as I get.

卡麥倫 ▸ 除了到陽明山泡溫泉之外，我好像沒機會到處去。我其實也比較喜歡在市區晃。偶爾我會到平時很少去的區域去走走，試試看沒去過的咖啡店或是餐廳，這樣對我來說就算是旅行了。

Sport event

運動比賽

大型的運動比賽有奧運（Olympic games）、亞運（Asian games）。或是台灣職棒大聯盟（Taiwan Major League）、美國職棒大聯盟（US Major League）、小聯盟（Minor League）、日本職棒（Nippon Professional Baseball）、摔角（Professional Wrestling）、相撲（Sumo Wrestling）、美國籃球（NBA）等等。一般學校的運動會（Sports carnival）、舞蹈比賽（Dance competition）、游泳比賽（Swimming competition），也都是運動比賽。運動比賽的勝負分為金牌得主（Gold Medalist）、銀牌得主（Silver medalist）、銅牌得主（Bronze medalist）。

雅思主題字彙表

❶ 奧運	olympic games
❷ 亞運	asian games
❸ 台灣職棒大聯盟	Taiwan Major League
❹ 美國職棒大聯盟	US Major League

❺ 小聯盟	minor League
❻ 日本職棒	Nippon Professional Baseball
❼ 摔角	Professional Wrestling
❽ 相撲	sumo wrestling
❾ 美國籃球	NBA
❿ 學校的運動會	Sports carnival
⓫ 舞蹈比賽	dance competition
⓬ 游泳比賽	swimming competition
⓭ 金牌得主	gold Medalist
⓮ 銀牌得主	silver medalist
⓯ 銅牌得主	bronze medalist
⓰ 殘障奧運	paralympic games
⓱ 田徑賽	track and field
⓲ 體操	gymnastic
⓳ 運動員的禁藥	performance-enhancing drug
⓴ 禁藥測試	drug Test

一問三答

Do you like to watch sports events live?

你喜歡看運動比賽的實況轉播嗎?

Josh ▸ Absolutely! Nothing is more exciting than a live sports event. I would go to the stadium if I could, but I don't live in New York, so there is no way that I can watch Yankees play in person. Live TV broadcasting is the next best thing! I normally watch the games with my friends in the house.

喬許 ▸ 那當然! 沒有什麼比看現場比賽更刺激的了! 如果可以的話，我當然想去體育館看現場，可是我又不住在紐約，沒有辦法現場看洋基隊比賽，能有實況轉播就很不錯了! 我通常會到我朋友家跟他一起看。

Abby ▸ Well, I am not a sports person, watching a sport event in live would be a torture for me. I don't get excited like the fans. I mean if it is an important sports event like

Olympic, I would be curious about whether Taiwan has won a match, but I won't stay up whole night just to watch it live.

艾比 ▸ 這個嘛，我不是很愛運動的人，看現場的運動比賽簡直就是要我的命，我不像運動迷們心情跟著起伏。如果是重要的比賽像奧運之類的，我當然會關心台灣是贏還是輸，可是我絕對不會熬夜來看實況轉播。

Cameron ▸ I do like to watch live sports events, but most of the time I've got work the next day, so I don't have the luxury to stay up late to watch the games. If I knew the game was going to be on in the early evening, then I would make an effort to watch it live.

卡麥倫 ▸ 我喜歡看實況轉播可是大部分的時間我隔天都要工作，所以不太可能有這個閒暇時間不睡覺來看比賽的。如果我知道轉播的時間是在下班時間以後的話，那我就會看轉播。

Weekend/ Free time

週末/休閒

週末是很多人唯一可以休息的時候，有的人喜歡趁這個機會運動，逛街，做平常沒機會做的事。有人喜歡趁這個機會休息（chill out）、補眠（sleep in）、追劇（watch soaps）、陪家人（spend time with family）、做家事（do chores）、去做臉（go to the day spa）、去兜風（go for a drive）、洗衣服（do laundry）、看漫畫（read comic books）、上課進修（take classes）、發呆（zone out）等等。週末很多人選擇外出旅遊，如果出外旅遊住房是旺季（high season），住房價格會偏高，而且觀光區（tourist attractions）人滿為患；淡季（low season）去反而比較有度假的品質。

雅思主題字彙表

❶ 休息	chill out
❷ 補眠	sleep in
❸ 追劇	watch soaps
❹ 陪家人	spend time with family

⑤ 旺季	high season
⑥ 觀光區	tourist attractions
⑦ 淡季	low season
⑧ 遛狗	walk the dog
⑨ 做家事	do chores
⑩ 整理東西	tidy things up
⑪ 去做臉或美體按摩	go to a day spa
⑫ 去兜風	go for a drive
⑬ 看電視	being a couch potato
⑭ 看漫畫	read comic books
⑮ 洗衣服	do Laundry
⑯ 上課進修	take classes
⑰ 發呆	zone out
⑱ 上健身房	go to the gym
⑲ 逛書局	browse the book store
⑳ 逛藥妝店	browse the pharmacy

一問三答

What do you normally do in your free time?

你有空的時候通常會做什麼?

Josh ▸ If the weather is good, then I will be at the beach, but if the weather is not right, then I will be at home playing video games! Video games are so addictive, so I lose track of time so easily. I can keep playing the whole night, if my mother didn't come and stop me.

喬許 ▸ 如果天氣不錯的話，那我就會去海邊，可是如果天氣不好，那我就會在家打電動。電玩這種東西真的很容易讓人上癮，我一開始打就會忘了時間，如果我媽沒有來叫我的話，我可以一直打下去。

Abby ▸ I will go shopping if I am free the whole day on the weekends. But if I only have an hour here and there. I would watch Korean soap instead. I stream them oneline, and I normally watch one or two episodes then I have to force myself to turn it off. Otherwise, I would run out of internet data in no time!

艾比 ▸ 如果我週末整天有空的話我就會去逛街，可是如果我只有零散的一兩個小時，那我就會上網下載韓劇。我通常只會看個一兩集就強迫關機，不然下載的容量很快就用完了。

Cameron ▸ Juggling between my girlfriend and my jobs is really tiring. My favorite thing to do in my spare time is actually doing nothing, just chilling out or catching up on sleeps.

卡麥倫 ▸ 平常要陪女朋友又要上班真的很累。我有空的時候最喜歡就是懶在那裡什麼都不做，不然就是補眠。

Color

顏色

彩虹的色調大家比較不熟的應該是靛色（indigo）與紫色（violet），還有一般常用卻不熟悉的顏色有：米白（beige）、蒂芬妮藍（turquoise）、深藍（navy blue）、酒紅色（burgundy）。顏色帶給人的感覺不同，深色通常令人覺得穩重（mature）、神秘（mysterious）、高貴（elegant）、嚴肅（solemn）。淺色則令人感覺輕鬆（relaxed）、活潑（upbeat）、正面（positive）、明亮（bright）、純真（naive ）等等。

雅思主題字彙表

❶ 靛色	indigo
❷ 紫色	violet
❸ 米白	beige
❹ 蒂芬妮藍	turquoise
❺ 深藍	navy blue
❻ 酒紅色	burgundy
❼ 穩重	mature

⑧ 神秘	mysterious
⑨ 高貴	elegant
⑩ 嚴肅	solemn
⑪ 輕鬆	relaxed
⑫ 活潑	upbeat
⑬ 正面	positive
⑭ 明亮	bright
⑮ 純真	naive
⑯ 很夏天的	summerly
⑰ 很有活力的	energetic
⑱ 膚色	skin tone
⑲ 襯托	complement
⑳ 污漬	stain

一問三答

Do you prefer to wear dark color or light color?

你比較喜歡穿深色或是淺色的衣服？

Josh ▸ I prefer to wear light colors, such as white or bright green. I spend a lot of time sun-bathing to get the tan I want, and I like to wear something that would complement my skin tone. I think light colors represent my personality as well. I am energetic and always positive.

喬許 ▸ 我喜歡穿淺色的衣服，像白色或是很亮的綠色之類。我好不容易才把我的皮膚曬成我想要的膚色，我當然要選擇可以襯托我膚色的顏色。我覺得淺色也很可以代表我的個性，我一直都是很有活力而且很正面的。

Abby ▸ I think it depends what kind of mood I am in. If I don't have any formal things to attend to that day, I will prefer to wear light color.

But if I have a formal meeting or something important on, then I will prefer to wear dark color just to look more professional.

艾比 ▸ 我覺得要看心情，如果我今天沒有什麼重要的事要處理，那我就想穿淺色的，可是如果我有會要開或是有重要的事，那我會選擇深色，這樣看起來比較專業。

Cameron ▸ I would prefer to wear dark colors because I need to visit my clients in the factory, and it is very likely to get grease or dirt on my shirt. If I wear a dark color shirt, I can hide the stains pretty well, but with a light color shirt, you can spot the stain from miles away. That's what I try to avoid.

卡麥倫 ▸ 我會喜歡穿深色，因為我常需要到廠房裡見客戶，廠房裡到處都是油汙，常會弄到衣服。所以如果我穿深色的，那污漬就看不太出來。如果換成是淺色衣服的話，那遠遠的就可以看到汙漬，我會盡量避免。

Computer

電腦

電腦的設備不斷地推陳出新，常見的電腦設備有螢幕（monitor）、主機（mother board）、鍵盤（keyboard）、無線滑鼠（optical Mouse）、印表機（printer）、掃描機（scanner）等等。每個需要使用電腦的理由不同，電腦的功能（functions）除了可以上網購物（online shopping）、打作業（assignment）、打線上遊戲（play online games）、聊天室（online chatroom）、線上論壇（online forum）、找資料（doing research）、下載節目（streaming）等等。電腦的種類也不侷限在桌上型電腦（desk top）、筆記型電腦（lap top），近年來平板電腦（tablet）、智慧型手機（smartphone）都很受歡迎，同時也具電腦的功能性。

雅思主題字彙表

❶ 螢幕	monitor
❷ 主機	mother board
❸ 鍵盤	keyboard

④ 無線滑鼠	optical mouse
⑤ 印表機	printer
⑥ 掃描機	scanner
⑦ 電腦的功能	functions
⑧ 上網購物	online shopping
⑨ 打作業	assignment
⑩ 打線上遊戲	play online games
⑪ 聊天室	online chatroom
⑫ 線上論壇	online forum
⑬ 找資料	doing research
⑭ 下載節目	streaming
⑮ 桌上型電腦	desktop
⑯ 筆記型電腦	lap top
⑰ 平板電腦	tablet
⑱ 智慧型手機	smartphone
⑲ 容量	capacity
⑳ 類格/下載時斷斷續續	lag

一問三答

How often do you use computer?

你用電腦的機會多嗎?

Josh ▸ I had to use computer almost everyday while I was a student, but since I graduated last year I have been spending lots of time at the beach. My computer is sitting on my desk gathering dusts as we speak. I hardly touch it now, and I check all my emails on my smartphone anyway.

喬許 ▸ 我還沒畢業之前我很常用電腦，可是去年畢業之後我大部分的時間都在海邊，我的電腦現在就丟在桌子上埋在厚厚的灰塵底下。我現在很少開電腦，我都用智慧型手機來看電子郵件。

Abby ▸ I use computer everyday at work for the corresponding between the company and our overseas suppliers. I will be in so much trouble, if the internet is not working because all emails would not come through properly. I can't live without the computer. I stream all my Korean soaps online with my lap top, too.

艾比 ▸ 我在公司每天都要用電腦跟國外供應商們連絡。如果網路當掉的話我就糟了，因為不知道是不是每封郵件都有收到。我沒有電腦就會活不下去了，因為我的手提電腦是拿來下載韓劇用的。

Cameron ▸ I don't use the desk top often but rely on my smartphone a lot because I am out and about visiting clients all the time. I do have to input the orders into the computer just for recordkeeping once every couple of days.

卡麥倫 ▸ 我不常用我的桌上型電腦，可是我很常用智慧型手機，因為我幾乎都在外面見客戶。我大概每隔幾天就要開電腦一次來輸入這幾天的訂單。

Movie

電影

電影的種類可以簡單分為喜劇（comedy）、驚悚片（thriller）、愛情片（romance）、劇情片（drama）、動作片（action）、科幻片（Si-Fi）、歷史片（historical）、動畫電影（animation movie）等等。票房好的電影（blockbuster）受歡迎的原因可以是因為劇情（storyline）好笑（Hilarious）、感人（Touching）、刺激（exciting）、令人意想不到的（unpredictable）等等。票房不好的原因可能是令觀眾覺得無聊或是劇情太誇張（exaggerating）、不合情理（doesn't make sense）、太肉麻/老套（too corny）、或是故事內容太過悲情（too depressing）。

雅思主題字彙表

❶ 喜劇	comedy
❷ 驚悚片	thriller
❸ 愛情片	romance
❹ 劇情片	drama
❺ 動作片	action

⑥ 科幻片	Si-Fi
⑦ 歷史片	historical
⑧ 動畫電影	animation movie
⑨ 賣座/票房好的電影	blockbuster
⑩ 劇情	storyline
⑪ 好笑	hilarious
⑫ 感人	touching
⑬ 刺激	exciting
⑭ 令人意想不到的	unpredictable
⑮ 太誇張	exaggerating
⑯ 不合情理	doesn't make sense
⑰ 太肉麻/老套	too corny
⑱ 太悲情	too depressing
⑲ 特殊效果	special effect
⑳ 續集	sequel

What kind of movie do you like the most?

你最喜歡看哪一類型的電影？

Josh ▸ I like to have a good laugh, so comedy is always my go to. My favorite is the "Hangover". It is about a group of friends deciding to go to Vegas to celebrate the bucks' night. They accidently got drugged so they had no recollection of what actually happened the night before. All they know is the groom is missing, and they have to find him in time for the wedding. It is hilarious, you've got to watch it.

喬許 ▸ 我覺得人生就是要開心，所以看電影我也喜歡看喜劇。我最喜歡的騙子就是"醉後大丈夫"。這部片子是在講有關一群朋友決定到拉斯維加斯去慶祝單身的最後一夜，但是他們卻意外地被下藥，完全不記得前晚發生過什麼事。他們只知道新郎不見了，一定要把他在婚禮前及時找回來。故事內容超搞笑的，大推!

Abby ▸ I love the girly movies, a sweet love story would be ideal. I also prefer a happy ending because most of the love stories in real life do not have fairytale endings. I think movie should not be too close to reality because life is hard enough as it is, why watch something that reminds you of how terrible life can be!

艾比 ▸ 我喜歡浪漫愛情片，最好就是很甜蜜的故事。我也喜歡皆大歡喜的結局，因為現實生活中很難真的有童話故事般的愛情。我覺得生活既然都那麼苦悶了，電影劇情就不應該太寫實，不然看了心情更糟。

Cameron ▸ I am a big fan of special effects and science fiction; I cannot resist the Si-Fi movies such as “Star wars” and “Avatar.” I think watching movies is a way to escape from reality, I always try to imagine I am one of the characters while I am watching the movie.

卡麥倫 ▸ 我超愛看有特效的故事，像星際大戰或是阿凡達那種科幻片我一定會去看。我覺得看電影就是要有想像空間，我總是一邊看一邊幻想我是電影裡的主題人物。

Unit 30 Vehicle 交通工具

在台灣最普遍的交通工具應該就是機車（scooter），有轎車的人口也不佔少數，以車款（make and model）來區別可以分為房車（sedan）、掀背車（hatchback）、休旅車（station wagon）、小貨車（ute）、多功能休旅車（SUV）。若是以大眾交通工具（public transportation）來説的話，除了公車之外，還有捷運（MRT/subway）、火車（train）、輕軌列車（light rail）、渡輪（ferry）和九人或十二人座的小巴（mini van）。也有頂級的交通工具，例如私人飛機（private jet）、直升機（helicopter）、私人遊艇（private yacht）等等。現在環保（environmental friendly）意識抬頭，腳踏車（push bike）也重新受到重視。

雅思主題字彙表

❶ 大眾交通工具	public transportation
❷ 捷運	MRT/ Subway
❸ 火車	train
❹ 輕軌列車	light rail

⑤ 渡輪	ferry
⑥ 房車	sedan
⑦ 掀背車	hatchback
⑧ 休旅車	station wagon
⑨ 小貨車	ute/pick up track
⑩ 多功能休旅車	SUV
⑪ 九人或十二人座的小巴	mini van
⑫ 車款	make and model
⑬ 私人飛機	private jet
⑭ 直升機	helicopter
⑮ 私人遊艇	private yacht
⑯ 環保	environmental friendly
⑰ 腳踏車	push bike
⑱ 機車	scooter
⑲ 大巴士	coach
⑳ 接駁巴士	shuttle bus

Do you own a vehicle?

你有沒有自己的交通工具?

Josh ▸ Yes, I do. I have a scooter, and in southern Taiwan that is all you need. There is not a lot of traffic in Heng Chuan, and unless you are going out of the town; otherwise, you don't really need a car. Scooters are perfect because they have very good fuel economy, and you don't need to worry about the parking.

喬許 ▸ 有，我有。我有一台機車。在南台灣機車就很夠用了。在恆春也沒有車潮，除非你要到別的縣市去，不然你也不需要開車。機車就最適合了，又省油又不用擔心停車的問題。

Abby ▸ Well, I don't own a car or a scooter, but I do have a push bike for my exercise routine on the weekends. Personally, I think there is no need to own a vehicle when you live in a city like Taipei. Owning a vehicle is more a hassle than a convenience when parking costs more than food!

艾比 ▸ 嗯，我沒有房車也沒有機車，可是我有一台腳踏車，是我用來周末假日健身用的。以我個人來說，我覺得我並不需要有車，尤其是住在像台北市這種地方。有車其實弊多於利，停車費比便當的錢都還貴呢!

Cameron ▸ Yeah, I've got a small car. It is a 2014 Mitsubishi Colt plus. I drive to work everyday, and all I need is a small car which is good on fuel. I bought it second hand from a car yard, but it comes with 6 months warranty. I bought it a year ago, and it hasn't caused any problems.

卡麥倫 ▸ 有的，我有一台小車。是 2014 年的三菱 Colt plus 車款。我每天都需要開車上班，所以省油的小車最適合我。我是在二手車場買的，還有含六個月的保固。我買了一年了，到現在都沒什麼問題。

Song

歌曲

歌曲除了情歌之外還有鄉村音樂（Country music）、重金屬（Heavy Metal）、沙發音樂（Lounge music）、拉丁情歌（Latino love songs）、流行歌（Pop music）、非主流音樂（Alternative）、饒舌樂（Rap）、個人的喜好不同（Each to their own）。以情歌來說，旋律（Melody）與歌詞（Lyric）常常很令人感動（Moving）、有時充滿了祝福（Blessing），有時是分手（Breakup）時離別（Separation）後又重聚（Reunited）。或是有第三者（Seeing someone else），被欺騙（Deceiving）後無奈（Nothing I can do）的心情，或是心碎了（Heartbroken），對對方充滿恨意（Hatred）等等。

雅思主題字彙表

❶ 鄉村音樂	country music
❷ 重金屬	heavy metal
❸ 沙發音樂	lounge music
❹ 拉丁情歌	latino love songs

⑤ 流行歌	pop music
⑥ 非主流音樂	alternative
⑦ 饒舌樂	rap
⑧ 個人的喜好不同	each to their own
⑨ 令人感動	moving
⑩ 祝福	blessing
⑪ 旋律	melody
⑫ 歌詞	lyric
⑬ 分手	breakup
⑭ 離別	separation
⑮ 重聚	reunited
⑯ 有第三者	seeing someone else
⑰ 欺騙	deceiving
⑱ 無奈	nothing I can do
⑲ 心碎	heartbroken
⑳ 恨意	hatred

一問三答

Q 31 Do you like to listen to love songs?

你喜歡聽情歌嗎？

Josh ▸ Love songs are not my cup of tea. I find most of the love songs are just corny and predictable. Either you like that girl but the girl doesn't love you back, or you are happily in love with someone. I am not ready to settle down with anyone just yet I guess that's why I can't really relate to it.

喬許 ▸ 情歌呢，真的不是我的菜。我覺得大部分的情歌都很老套又一成不變，不是你愛那個女孩而那個女孩不愛你，就是目前戀愛 ING。我目前還不想定下來，可能是這樣我對情歌真的沒什麼感覺。

Abby ▸ I love the love songs because I always imagine I will meet my Mr. Right one day and live happily ever after just like what the lyrics say. Obviously, my Mr. Right is still waiting to be found, but listening to love songs keeps me positive about finding true love one day.

艾比 ▸ 我很喜歡聽情歌，因為我總是幻想著有一天我會遇到我的真命天子，過得幸福美滿，就像歌詞裡寫的一樣。雖然我的真命天子目前還沒出現，可是聽著情歌會讓我對未來充滿希望，我相信我總有一天會找到他的!

Cameron ▸ I don't mind love songs because some of them really touch me heart especially when my ex-girlfriend decided to walk out on me a couple of years ago. I was very upset because we were almost engaged. The sad love songs did save me from the misery.

卡麥倫 ▸ 我不介意聽情歌，因為有些歌我覺得寫得很好，很有共鳴。尤其是幾年前我剛跟我前女友分手的時候，我很低潮，因為我們差一點就訂婚了。聽傷心的情歌來抒發心情，我也慢慢走出來了。

Photograph

照片

以輸出的方式照片可以分為紙本照片（hardcopy）、相簿（album）、電子版（soft copy）、無框畫（canvas）等等，色調上可以做調整，像 黑白（black and white）、彩色（colored）、復古（retro）色調。照片的主題可以是人物寫真（portrait）、風景（scenery）、夜景（night view）、戶外全景（landscape）、網拍商品（merchandise）。相框（photo frame）及護貝（lamination）逐漸地失去重要性，因為越來越多人選擇用電腦來儲存照片，因為修圖（air-brush）很方便。而底片（negatives）這種東西也快要被數位單眼相機（digital SLR）取代了。有些人會特別將照片剪貼成冊做成具有紀念性的剪貼簿（scrapbooking）。

雅思主題字彙表

❶ 紙本照片	hardcopy
❷ 相簿	album
❸ 電子版	soft copy
❹ 無框畫	canvas

❺ 黑白	black and white
❻ 彩色	colored
❼ 復古	retro
❽ 人物寫真	portrait
❾ 風景	scenery
❿ 夜景	night view
⓫ 全景	landscape
⓬ 商品	merchandise
⓭ 相框	photo frame
⓮ 護貝	lamination
⓯ 剪貼簿	scrapbooking
⓰ 修圖	airbrush
⓱ 底片	Negatives
⓲ 數位單眼相機	Digital SLR
⓳ 鏡頭	Lens
⓴ 閃光燈	Flash light

Do you prefer to take photos of others or being in the photo?

你比較喜歡照相還是幫人拍照?

Josh ▸ Well, I spend a lot of time and effort making sure I look the way I am, of course I would like to show off my looks as much as I can. I update my Facebook profile photo everyday with my daily selfie! Some people might think I love myself a bit too much, but I love being in photos.

喬許 ▸ 嗯，我花了很多時間與精力來維持我的外表，我當然想曝光率高一點啊!我每天都會上傳自拍照更新臉書的大頭照，有些人覺得我實在太自戀了，可是我真的很喜歡看到我自己的照片。

Abby ▸ Taking photos to me is like creating memories for different occasions. I cherish every moment with my friends and families, and I like to be in the photos with them. I like to print the photos out and look at them from time to time. People always remember who is in the photo, but no one would remember who took that photo!

艾比 ▸ 我覺得照片是用來留下回憶用的，我很珍惜跟家人朋友在一起的時刻，所以我喜歡跟他們一起出現在照片中。我會把照片都洗出來，偶爾會拿出來翻閱。大家都只會記得照片中的人，不會有人記得照片是誰照的!

Cameron ▸ I don't like being in the photos because I think I am not photogenic at all. To be honest, I think I look terrible in most of my photos although my mother says I look good. I much prefer being the photographer instead. I think taking photos of nice plates of food is much more fun than taking photos of myself.

卡麥倫 ▸ 我不喜歡出現在照片中，因為我很不上相。雖然我媽都說照片很好看，可是說真的我覺得我每張照片都很醜，所以我情願當幕後的攝影師，我覺得拍食物都比拍我自己來得有趣。

TV program

電視節目

打開電視就可以發現電視節目的類型琳瑯滿目，在國外很常見的是實境秀（reality TV）在台灣最受歡的可能就是綜藝節目（variety shows）了，或是以選秀為主的歌唱比賽（singing competition）、舞蹈比賽（dancing competition）。與時事相關的新聞節目（News channel）、政論節目（political commentary shows）、談話型節目（talk shows）、紀錄片（documentary）也很受歡迎。另外還有 MTV 台、運動比賽轉播（live sports channel）、美食節目（food shows）、烹調節目（cooking shows）、卡通（cartoons）兒童節目（kids shows）、電視購物（shopping channels）、連續劇（soaps）、布袋戲（Taiwanese puppet show）、歌仔戲（Taiwanese opera）、電影台（Movie channel）、電視影集（TV series）等等。

雅思主題字彙表

❶ 實境秀	reality TV
❷ 綜藝節目	variety shows

③ 歌唱比賽	singing competition
④ 舞蹈比賽	dancing competition
⑤ 政論節目	political commentary shows
⑥ 談話型節目	talk shows
⑦ 紀錄片	documentary
⑧ 運動比賽轉播	live sports channel
⑨ 美食節目	food shows
⑩ 烹調節目	cooking shows
⑪ 卡通	cartoons
⑫ 兒童節目	kids shows
⑬ 電視購物	shopping channels
⑭ 連續劇	soaps
⑮ 布袋戲	Taiwanese puppet show
⑯ 歌仔戲	Taiwanese opera
⑰ 新聞節目	News channel
⑱ 電影台	Movie channel
⑲ 電視影集	TV series
⑳ 行腳節目	travel shows

一問三答

Q 33 What is your favorite TV program?

你最喜歡看什麼電視節目？

Josh ▸ I love to watch American TV series. My favorite show is "Friends". It is not the latest series, but it is the classic all-time favorite. It is all about love triangles and friendships among 6 friends. The storyline is funny and easy to follow. The best thing is, I picked up a lot of slang from watching the series.

喬許 ▸ 我很愛看美國的電視影集，我最喜歡的是"六人行"。這不是最新的，但卻是最經典，最受人喜歡的一套影集。內容是有關這六個好友之間的感情糾結還有誠摯的友誼。劇情很好笑，也很容易看懂。最棒的是看了這個影集我還學到很多英文的俗語。

Abby ▸ My favorite program on TV is actually the shopping channel. I know they are just sales presentations, but I like to know what is the in thing at the moment. If I saw something I like, I would order the product because they offer 10 days free trial and guarantee your money back. There is no risk of wasting money, other than the hassle of arranging for return collection.

艾比 ▸ 我最喜歡的電視節目其實是購物頻道，我知道那不過就是賣東西而已，可是看一下現在在流行什麼也好。如果我看到我喜歡的東西，我也是會買，因為它有十天鑑賞期，還保證退款，我覺得沒什麼浪費錢的風險，只是要安排退貨比較麻煩而已。

Cameron ▸ I like to watch the News channel because I think the Taiwanese News channel is quite entertaining. The news coverage not only includes serious stuff like suicide bombing, but also funny stories like where would be the best spot for Pokemon Go! I watch news everyday, so I won't run out of conversation topics with my clients.

卡麥倫 ▸ 我喜歡看新聞台因為我覺得台灣的新聞台很有娛樂性。新聞裡不只有像人肉炸彈這種嚴肅的新聞事件，還會告訴你寶可夢要去哪裡抓比較好。我每天都會看新聞，這樣我才有話題可以跟客戶聊天。

Fashion/ Clothing
穿著

以男裝的衣服款式來說有西裝外套（jacket）、襯衫（shirt）、西裝褲（paints）、短褲（shorts）、涼鞋（sandal）、球鞋（sneakers）、拖鞋（flip flop）等等。比較特別的女裝則有細肩帶上衣（singlet）、無袖上衣（tan top）、無肩帶上衣（tube top）等等。衣服的剪裁有: 合身款（loose fit）、貼身款（slim fit）。衣服的布料（material）也有很多選擇，例如棉布（cotton）、羊毛（wool）、雪紡紗（chiffon）、燈心絨（corduroy）。提到衣著就不能忘了飾品，常見的配件有手環（bracelet）、項鍊（necklace）。

雅思主題字彙表

❶ 西裝外套	jacket
❷ 襯衫	shirt
❸ 西裝褲	paints
❹ 短褲	shorts
❺ 涼鞋	sandal
❻ 球鞋	sneakers

⑦ 拖鞋	flip flop
⑧ 細肩帶上衣	singlet
⑨ 無袖上衣	tan top
⑩ 無肩帶的上衣	tube top
⑪ 合身款	loose fit
⑫ 貼身款	slim fit
⑬ 質料	material
⑭ 棉布	cotton
⑮ 羊毛	wool
⑯ 雪紡紗	chiffon
⑰ 燈心絨	corduroy
⑱ 配件	accessory
⑲ 手環	bracelet
⑳ 項鍊	necklace

一問三答

What type of clothes do you normally wear?

你平常的穿著打扮是怎樣?

Josh ▸ I pretty much wear T-shirt and board shorts everyday because I don't need to worry about dressing up for work. The weather in Heng Chuan is always hot and humid, even the winter is really mild. All you need is a long sleeve jacket. I do have a wind breaker for my scooter ride. I don't think I own a lot of thick winter clothing.

喬許 ▸ 我幾乎每天都是 T 恤加海灘褲，因為我不需要去上班要穿什麼。而且恆春的天氣又濕又熱，就算冬天也不是太冷，大概加件長袖夾克就可以。要騎機車的時候我會穿風衣，我其實沒什麼冬天的衣服。

Abby ▸ I normally wear a dress to work on week days, but on the weekends I like to wear something more casual, maybe shorts and singlet. If the weather is a bit windy then I will put on jeans and slim fit jacket. I like wearing high heels because it just looks sexy.

艾比 ▸ 如果是要上班的時候我通常是穿洋裝，可是週末的話我就穿得隨便一點，大概是細肩帶上衣加熱褲。如果風有點大的話，我就換牛仔長褲還有合身的夾克。我還喜歡配高跟鞋因為我覺得看起來很性感。

Cameron ▸ Business shirt with work pants is my standard outfit because I need to look professional for work. If I need to go and visit clients, then I might put on a tie. I don't often wear a jacket because it is too warm in Taiwan. I get really sweaty if I wear one.

卡麥倫 ▸ 我的標準穿著就是襯衫加西裝褲，因為上班的關係，需要穿得正式一點。如果我還需要去見客戶的話，那我會再加條領帶。我通常不會穿西裝外套，因為台灣的天氣實在太熱了，我如果穿的話會汗流浹背。

Food

食物

在台灣早餐店常見早餐種類有蛋餅（omelette pancake）、煎餃/鍋貼（pot sticker）、蒸餃（steam dumplings）、蘿蔔糕（radish cake）、捲餅（wraps）等等。中式午餐晚餐的選擇如也不少，例如火鍋（hot pot/ steam boat）、乾麵（dry noodles）、餛飩湯（wonton soup）、便當（bento box），米糕（sticky rice）、碗粿（rice cake）。喜歡西餐的還有義大利麵（pasta）、千層麵（lasagne）、牛排（steak）、羊排（lamp chops）、豬排（pork chops）等等。不管喜歡吃什麼，衛生（hygienic）才是最重要的，要是吃了肚子不舒服（It doesn't agree with me）或是食物中毒（food poisoning）、拉肚子（diarrhea）的話，就算再美味下次也不會再光臨 。

雅思主題字彙表

❶ 蛋餅	omelette pancake
❷ 煎餃/鍋貼	pot sticker
❸ 蒸餃	steam dumplings

❹ 蘿蔔糕	radish cake
❺ 捲餅	wraps
❻ 火鍋	hot pot/ steam boat
❼ 乾麵	dry noodles
❽ 餛飩湯	wonton soup
❾ 便當	bento box
❿ 米糕	sticky rice
⓫ 碗粿	rice cake
⓬ 義大利麵	pasta
⓭ 千層麵	lasagne
⓮ 牛排	steak
⓯ 羊排	lamp chops
⓰ 豬排	pork chops
⓱ 衛生	hygienic
⓲ 吃了肚子不舒服	it doesn't agree with me
⓳ 食物中毒	food poisoning
⓴ 拉肚子	diarrhea

Q 35 What is your favorite food?

你最喜歡吃什麼東西?

Josh ▸ I love to go to this hawkers' food stall right by Heng Chuan bus terminal because they got the best oyster omelette. They get the freshly harvested oysters from Tong Kang everyday, and they have a secret recipe for their omelette sauce. I go there at least once a week.

喬許 ▸ 我最喜歡恆春車站旁邊的小吃的蚵仔煎，他們的蚵仔煎最棒了！他們每天都從東港運來現撈的鮮蚵，再加上他們的特殊醬料，我至少一個星期要去報到一次。

Abby ▸ I actually really like fried chicken and chips. I know they are not the healthiest choices for food but they are just so tasty. Most of the time my diet is pretty healthy, I eat plenty of fresh fruit and vegetables but when I feel like a midnight snack, that is the first thing that comes to mind.

艾比 ▸ 我其實很喜歡吃炸雞跟薯條，我知道這很不健康可是他們真的很美味。我大部分都吃得很健康，我吃很多新鮮蔬菜跟水果。可是如果有半夜嘴巴有點饞的時候，我第一個想吃的就是炸雞跟薯條。

Cameron ▸ My favorite food is dumplings. I like them whether they are fried, steamed, or boiled. My favorite flavor is the port and chive one. It goes really well with a bit of soy sauce and vinegar dipping sauce. Some people like to add fresh ginger in the sauce, but I just find it too strong.

卡麥倫 ▸ 我最喜歡吃餃類了，不管是煎餃、蒸餃還是水餃我都喜歡。我最愛的口味是豬肉韭菜，這跟油醋醬油沾醬很搭。有些人喜歡加一點新鮮的薑絲，可是我覺得這樣味道太濃了。

Unit 36 Game

遊戲

小時候玩遊戲的機會最多，常見的遊戲有拔河（tug-of-war）、老師說（simon says） 跳房子（hopscotch）、捉迷藏（hide and seek）、抓鬼（tag）、猜拳（paper, scissors, stone）、跳繩（jump rope）、紅綠燈（red light, green light）、打彈珠（marbles）等等。長大玩遊戲的機會可能是學校聯誼的破冰遊戲（ice breaking games）或是公司訓練的團隊建立遊戲（team bonding games）、夜店遊戲真心話大冒險（truth and dare）等等。既然是遊戲就有輸贏，比分數（score）高低，或是平手（it is a tight），輸的一方要接受處罰（punishment）。

雅思主題字彙表

❶ 拔河	tug-of-war
❷ 老師說	simon says
❸ 跳房子	hopscotch
❹ 捉迷藏	hide and seek
❺ 抓鬼	tag

⑥ 猜拳	paper, scissors, stone
⑦ 跳繩	jump rope
⑧ 紅綠燈	red light, green light
⑨ 打彈珠	marbles
⑩ 破冰遊戲	ice breaking games
⑪ 團隊建立遊戲	team bonding games
⑫ 真心話大冒險	truth and dare
⑬ 玩泥巴	making mud pies
⑭ 抓蝌蚪	catching Tadpoles
⑮ 爬樹	climbing trees
⑯ 醫生遊戲	play doctor and patient
⑰ 換裝遊戲	play dress up
⑱ 平手	it is a tight
⑲ 分數	score
⑳ 處罰方式	punishment

What was your favorite game when you were little?

你小時候最喜歡的遊戲是什麼？

Josh ▸ My favorite game was hide and seek. We used to play it with all the kids from the neighborhood in front of the temple. I was pretty good at the game. I loved to hide right behind the big banyan tree, and the funny thing is that no one seems to know to look there!

喬許 ▸ 我以前最喜歡玩躲貓貓了，我常常跟鄰居的小孩們在廟口玩。我還蠻厲害的，我最喜歡躲在大榕樹的後面，很奇怪就沒人會去那裏找。

Abby ▸ When I was little, I love to play tea party with my sister, we would bring out all the bears and dollies and pretend they were guests in our castle. We would dress them up as princess and feed them imaginary cake or biscuits. It sounds silly now, but I loved it when I was a kid.

艾比 ▸ 我小時候最喜歡跟我妹妹玩家家酒，我們還會把小熊跟娃娃都拿出來把他們當成來訪我們城堡的客人，我們還會幫他們穿衣服，扮成公主，再請他們吃假裝的蛋糕還有餅乾。現在說起來好像很蠢，可是我小時候真的超愛的！

Cameron ▸ I always carried marbles with me when I was little. I was obsessed about playing marbles, I took them everywhere with me. I still remember I played marbles with my classmates during recess at school everyday. I had a whole collection of them, big ones and little ones, you name it.

卡麥倫 ▸ 我小時候隨身都會帶著彈珠，我真的很迷打彈珠這回事，無論到哪裡都堅持要帶著。我還記得每天只要下課鐘聲響，我就會跟同學去玩彈珠。我蒐集了很多彈珠，有大的有小的，只要你說的出來我幾乎都有。

雅思口語第二部分

學習進度表

- ☐ Unit 01 新聞
- ☐ Unit 02 湖泊/河川
- ☐ Unit 03 電器
- ☐ Unit 04 重要的決定
- ☐ Unit 05 音樂
- ☐ Unit 06 國家
- ☐ Unit 07 廣告
- ☐ Unit 08 幫助
- ☐ Unit 09 汙染
- ☐ Unit 10 國家的問題
- ☐ Unit 11 書籍
- ☐ Unit 12 難忘的情境
- ☐ Unit 13 卡通/故事人物
- ☐ Unit 14 名人
- ☐ Unit 15 節慶

是否能於考場中獲取理想成績？

★ 完成 8 單元 ▶可能

★ 完成 12 單元 ▶較有可能

★ 完成 15 單元 ▶一定可以

新聞故事

請描述一段讓你覺得印象深刻的新聞故事

新聞一｜停車留言 Message on the windscreen

為停車位爭吵是常見的事，這位住戶連續幾天看到一台沒見過的車停在他常停的車位，他實在受不了了就寫了張字條夾在那台車的擋風玻璃上，說：這個車位是給住戶停的，你不是住戶！結果隔天早上他又看見那台車，擋風玻璃上多了一張字條說：我是你的新鄰居，我剛剛搬來！

新聞二｜為了救小孩殺了大猩猩 Kill the gorilla to save the kid

美國有個小孩和媽媽逛動物園時，不小心掉進了大猩猩的柵欄裡。大猩猩將小孩從護城河中抓出來，抱在懷裡。因為麻醉針可能會讓大猩猩獸性大發而傷害小孩，為了救出小孩，園方決定槍殺大猩猩。可是大猩猩何其無辜。

新聞三｜日本的猴子愛泡溫泉 Hot spring monkeys

在日本北海道有一個奇觀，就是雪猴泡溫泉。因為氣候寒冷，冰天雪地裡雪猴群們也就地取材，一隻隻跳進現成的溫泉裡。溫泉裡的猴子有大有小，完全不怕人。他們臉上的表情真的好享受，真是蔚為奇觀。沒有親看到還真是難以想像。

新聞四｜小孩不見了 Missing kid

有一對日本爸媽因為生氣小孩不守規矩，想要嚇嚇小孩看他會不會收斂一點，經過山區時就在半路上，叫小孩下車反省。父母隔一陣子回來找小孩，卻發現小孩不見了，報警了又怕丟臉，不敢跟警察講實話。還好最後小孩找到了，山區有熊出沒呢！

新聞五｜載大熊回家 The giant Teddy

幾年前有家賣場推出巨大的絨毛玩具熊，一隻只要台幣一千塊。很多年輕人瘋狂搶購，這也造成了騎機車載絨毛大熊回家的窘境，還有人因為車裡塞不下，直接把熊綁在車頂。回到家更糟糕，發現熊太大沒位子放，又要載回去退錢！

新聞六｜新加坡的再生水 Newater

新加坡地密人稠，水資源都要向鄰近的馬來西亞購買。為了減少對馬來西亞的依賴，新加坡也不斷研發再生水資源的能力，除了海水淡化還有雨水蒐集之外，新水 (Newater) 則是由汙水淨化而再生成飲用水，可是想到要把汙水喝下肚，心裡真是有點掙扎。

新聞七｜川普選總統 Trump runs for president

剛開始聽到川普要選美國總統，我相信很多人都把他當個笑話看。他是個成功的商人，可是他並沒有政治經驗。沒想到後來他的聲勢看漲，連希拉蕊都要擔心爭不過他。其實把國家當企業管理可能也不是件壞事，只是他提出的政見能真正執行多少還很難說呢！

新聞八｜世界末日的預言 Armageddon

每隔幾年就會有人出來說他預言世界末日將到來，要世人提早準備。叫人要買組合貨櫃屋，還要積存糧食。他精準地指出世界末日的日期還有時間，甚至連幾分幾秒都告訴你。可是當他的預言沒有實現，那個預言家卻是一副沒事發生的樣子。

Q1 Describe a story you heard or read about in the news that made an impression.

MP3 37

請描述一段讓你印象深刻的新聞故事

印度能吃的餐具 Edible cutlery

I read this story in the newspaper once. This India inventor created an edible spoon which is made of a combination of millet, rice, and wheat. It looks just like a normal wooden spoon, but it is totally biodegradable.

我曾經在報紙上讀到，有一個印度的發明家，他用小米、白米還有麥子混和做出了可以吃的湯匙。那個湯匙看起來跟一般的木湯匙沒兩樣，可是卻是可以腐化分解的。

He first got this idea from knowing how much plastic cutlery is wasted each year and it just keeps piling up. Plastic does not degrade in a nature environment, plus, it is not as safe as we thought because plastic is a

他靈感的來源是發現原來一年裡面被丟棄的塑膠餐具這麼的多，而且數量每一年不停地增加。塑膠在自然環境裡面不會腐化分解而且塑膠也

chemical complex. Toxic substance will be released into food when the conditions are right, such as high temperatures or contact with oil.

不是我們想像中的那麼安全，因為那是種化學合成物，毒素會藉由高溫或是跟油質接觸時而溶解到食物裡。

Therefore, an edible one would be just the solution. His edible spoons even come in different flavors to compliment different dishesthat you can choose from: plain, sweet or savory. I think it is really clever!

所以發明可以吃的湯匙就是最好的解決辦法了。他的湯匙還有分不同口味來搭配不同的食物，有原味、甜的或是鹹的，我覺得實在很酷！

However, his business did not take off rapidly. Although he has the perfect recipe and idea to make the edible cutlery, the cost of the making it is so much higher than making plastic cutlery. India is known as a poor country; the majority of the population cannot afford edible cutlery. He would have to market his environmental

可是他的生意並沒有大展鴻圖，雖然他有很棒的配方和想法來做出可以吃的餐具，可是他卻沒有辦法把這個餐具做的跟塑膠餐具一樣便宜。在大家印象裡，印度是一個蠻窮苦的國家，大部分的人口負

friendly product to a different consumer group.

擔不起可以吃的餐具。他必須要另外找客戶群。

I think he should promote the idea in the western countries where there is more environmental awareness. It might make his business more sustainable.

我覺得他應該到西方國家去推廣，他們也比較有環保意識。這樣他生意才可能可以持續下去。

湖泊/河川

請描述一個你曾去過或是想去的湖泊或河川

湖泊一｜嘉明湖 Chia-Ming Lake

我從高中時期就一直想去嘉明湖。嘉明湖位於台東縣，他有個很美的名字叫天使的眼淚，因為不管從哪個角度看，湖面總是湛藍的。可是因為嘉明湖有很多可怕的鬼故事，所以我也一直約不到人想要一起去挑戰。不知道這輩子會不會有機會去。

湖泊二｜曾文水庫 Tseng-Wen Reservoir

我國小的時候因為參加童軍團的關係，曾經去台南縣的曾文水庫露營。曾文水庫是台灣最大的人工湖，也是影響嘉南平原供水的重要水庫。壩頂的風景很壯觀，群山環繞非常的美麗。我印象最深刻的是滿天星斗的夜晚，那是我第一次看過這麼多星星。

湖泊三 | 日月潭 Sun-Moon Lake

去年夏天爸爸決定帶爺爺奶奶出去走一走，所以我們決定到南投的日月潭來個家族旅行。我們的飯店房間可以看到湖景，傍晚的時候湖上升起濃濃的霧氣，感覺好像置身仙境。隔天早上我們搭船去環湖，經過導遊的解說才知道原來日月潭一邊是日潭，一邊叫月潭，所以才有日月潭之稱。

湖泊四 | 大學池 University lake

幾個月前我跟我男朋友去溪頭玩，溪頭有一座有名的湖叫做大學池。大學池上有一座竹子搭的橋叫情人橋，跟男朋友去更是要去走一下。大學池被濃濃的樹林圍住，湖面的反射時而藍、時而綠實在很特別。我最喜歡太陽光透過樹梢映在湖面的感覺。

湖泊/河川五 | 碧潭 Bitan scenic area

趁假日的時候我跟媽媽上台北去探望妹妹，她帶我們到新店的碧潭玩。碧潭周圍有很多餐廳，我們在那裏喝下午茶享受碧潭的風光。突然間，媽媽說她年輕的時候碧潭是自殺聖地，很多人從吊橋上一躍而下，我的背脊忽然涼了一下，還真希望她沒告訴我。

湖泊/河川六｜蓮池潭 Lotus Lake

上個星期我帶我的爺爺奶奶到高雄的蓮池潭玩，蓮池潭上有兩座有名的建築物叫龍虎塔，龍虎塔裡有很多有關勸世的壁畫，習俗相信從龍口進，虎口出可以消災解厄，所以我們也去體驗一下。蓮池潭上的建築物充滿濃濃的中國風，我覺得國外旅客會很喜歡。

湖泊/河川七｜大豹溪 Dabao River

在新聞上常常聽到位於台北三峽的大豹溪又發生溺水事件。讓我好奇的是大豹溪到底有多美，為什麼這麼多人會想去那裡玩，我實在很想去看看。聽說它的風景媲美花東縱谷，有很多奇特的岩石沖刷景觀，也許明後年我會約幾個好朋友特別去看看。

湖泊/河川八｜愛河 Love River

我最喜歡跟女朋友到高雄愛河了，尤其是晚上河邊的感覺。每每都有街頭藝人表演，還有浪漫的音樂。跟我小時候比起來，愛河的汙染減少了很多，我們現在有時會搭船去遊河，順便欣賞高雄港的美景，真不愧是約會聖地。

Q2 Describe a lake or river that visited or wish to visit.

MP3 38

請描述一個你曾去過或是想去的湖泊或河川

水漾森林 Mystery swampy forest

There is this secrete location in Chai-Yi County near Ali Mountain that not many people know about. There is this beautiful dammed lake that was caused by the 921 earthquake. What's special about this lake is, the trees were trapped in the flood slowly losing their leaves and dying eventually, and all the dead tree trucks stick out of the lakes like the telephone poles. It looks amazing with the blue sky and the reflection of the lake. People call this place "Mystery swampy forest."

在 921 大地震後，嘉義縣阿里山鄉出現了一個秘境，一座因為地震阻斷溪流而產生的堰塞湖，這個湖特別的地方是，湖裡原有的樹因為泡在水裡而死亡，只留下一根根像電線桿的樹幹從水中竄出，配合藍天及湖水的倒影，大家稱這個地方為水漾森林。

Around 10 years While the club members of mountain hiking

大概是十年前我還在念大學的時候，

were planning a trip to the "Mystery swampy forest." I was very tempted, but unfortunately it was only open to club members, so I missed out on the opportunity.

登山社的同學計畫要到水漾森林去。我很有興趣可是因為只有開放給社員，所以我就錯過了。

I was told you have to be fit to be able to make it because it would take 5-6 hours on foot in the winding mountain trail and occasionally there were vertical climbs.

有人告訴我要去水漾森林需要很有體力，因為大概要走 5-6 小時的山路，偶而還有垂直的攀爬。

I am quite a small person, and I doubt if I would be able to carry all the gears with me and walk such a long way. I know the view would probably be worth it, but the moment I think about I have to walk another 5-6 hours to get back. The reality starts to sink in.

我不算高大，我懷疑我真的有辦法背那麼重的行囊走那麼遠嗎？ 我知道美景應該很值得看，可是一想到回程又是 5-6 個小時，我就怕了。

I watched a documentary about it not long ago, and it was saying the water level there is

不久前我看了一段紀錄片，說水漾森林的水位急速減少，

dropping dramatically. I do wish I could visit the lake before it disappears completely.

我希望在它完全消失之前有機會去看。

電器

請描述一樣讓你生活更便利的電器

電器一｜電視 Television

電視可以把世界帶到我眼前，無論是韓劇、港劇、娛樂新聞還是世界新聞，我不需要出門，只要打開電視就可以看到，而且非常具時效性。無論世界的角落發生了什麼大事，新聞都會馬上插播，不像報紙一旦出版後就沒有辦法更新。

電器二｜洗衣機 Washing machine

把衣服跟洗衣粉放進去，輕輕按一下設定，衣服就幫你洗得乾乾淨淨，而且還有脫水功能，非常省時省力。衣服在洗的同時我還可以坐下來喝咖啡吃點心。我不用像奶奶那個年代帶著水桶還有洗衣板到河邊一件一件敲打搓洗，再扛著濕衣服回家曬。

電器三｜電鍋 Rice cooker

電鍋煮出來的飯又香又軟，而且最棒的是我不用在旁邊監看火侯。只要插電就可以恆溫，更可以預設定時。中學露營的時候我們要學用柴火還有湯鍋煮飯 ，一下擔心火太大，一下擔心水太少，還要怕沒悶熟。等飯煮好鍋底已經焦了。

電器四｜冰箱 Refrigerator

如果沒有冰箱我真的不知道該如何保存食物，尤其是像肉品、鮮奶這種容易腐敗的東西。剩菜廚餘也必須要丟棄，這樣會造成很多的浪費。誰有空天天到市場買菜煮三餐，都不用上班了嗎？ 冰箱真的是個很棒的發明，而且是每個人都會需要的產品。

電器五｜吹風機 Hair dryer

按照華人古時候的傳統，女人坐月子的時候是不能洗頭的，很可能是因為水質的問題無法控管，還有沒有辦法立即吹乾可能會為產婦帶來疾病。吹風機真的是女性的福音，尤其是在寒冷的冬天。頭髮又不能不洗，如果沒有趕快吹乾真的很不舒服。

電器六｜吸塵器 Vacuum

在吸塵器發明之前，打掃地毯真的是個噩夢！ 只能用掃的或是拿到室外用特別的地毯刷子，一邊打一邊刷。清潔效果非常有限，而且塵蹣細菌根本都清除不掉，衛生上有很大的疑慮。吸塵器真的是造福人群的發明，不然那些對塵蹣過敏的人該怎麼辦呢？

電器七｜電腦 computer

現在的學生應該連打字機長什麼樣子都沒看過，其實就是桌上型電腦的前身。電腦真的是跨時代的發明。現在生活中的每個環節幾乎都跟電腦有關。就連去餐廳吃飯，也是用電腦點餐。電腦可以互相連線，對於資料的整合實在太方便了，不用人工一個一個比對。

電器八｜行動電源 Power bank

行動電源對我來說太重要了！ 我這種整天滑手機的人，電池根本就不夠用。以前我隨身帶電源線，只要有機會，不管到哪裡都會把手機拿出來充電。自從有了行動電源之後，我就不用到處找插座，這樣我女朋友也不會找不到我了！

Q3 Please describe a piece of electronic equipment which made your life easier.

MP3 39

請描述一樣讓你生活更便利的電器

智慧型手機 Smartphone

Where shall I start with my smartphone? Smartphone is everything in one! It is a phone, a camera, a calculator, a computer and so much more!

我該從何說起呢？智慧型手機簡直是集所有優點於一身，它是手機，也是相機，計算機還是台電腦呢！還有其他數不清的功能。

I was not a smartphone user until pretty late. I was a bit resentful about learning new technology.

我不是一開始就是個智慧型手機的支持者，剛開始我也很排斥新科技。

Before I got my first smartphone, I didn't understand why

在我拿到第一支智慧型手機之前，我

people get addicted to their phone, but now I can't live without my phone.

不懂為什麼有人會對手機上癮，可是我現在真的不能沒有我的手機。

I have to check my emails when I am out and about for work. I had to bring my laptop with me everywhere I went before, but all I need now is my smartphone. If I want to scan some information to share with my coworker, all I have to do is take a photo with my smartphone then send it as an attachment in my email. This is definitely revolutionary !

我在外面出差時需要不斷地察看電子郵件，以前我到哪裡都一定要帶我的筆記型電腦，現在我只需要我的手機，就算我需要掃描文件給我的同事看，我也只要拿手機照張相，然後用郵件附件傳出去。這真是太劃時代了！

My favorite function is skype. I can check on my boyfriend all the time. If I wasn't sure whether he is telling me the truth, I will get him to put skype on, so I can see where he is. Who would have thought this is what I use Skype for !

我最喜歡的功能其實是 Skype 視訊，我隨時隨地都可以查我男朋友在哪裡。如果我覺得他沒有講實話，我就叫他開視訊，讓我看看他在哪裡。沒有人想到視訊可以這樣用吧！

But the thing is, convenience does not come cheap. I spent about 1000 NTD a month in phone bills; otherwise, I would not have enough data to do what I want to do. Luckily, I am not obsessed about having to have the latest model; otherwise, it would cost more !

可是科技的方便性真的不便宜，我一個月大概要花台幣一千元來繳電話費，不然我的網路容量不夠。還好我是不堅持一定要最新款的手機，不然開銷會更大！

重要的決定

請描述一個你人生中重要的決定

決定一｜升學或就業 Work or study

大學畢業前夕，我一直在考慮是否該投入職場，可是我並不確定我自己要找怎樣的工作，我又不想只做基層的工作，又擔心沒有碩士學位以後無法升遷。最後在爸爸的建議下我決定去念碩士。可是念了碩士之後，我發現找工作卻沒有我想像的順利，其實有點後悔。

決定二｜出國留學 Study aboard

我從小就一直想要出國留學，不是我對台灣的教育沒有信心，而是我想增加自己的國際經驗，還有拓展眼界。其實我也有點擔心出國念書會跟台灣社會有斷層，可是評估過後還是覺得利多於弊，畢竟增加英文能力對我回來就業會有很大的幫助。

決定三 | 買房子 Buying a house

畢業後工作也五六年了，存了一筆小錢，打算拿來當頭期款買房子。雖然不太夠，可是有爸媽贊助一些也還可以。但是一想到從此之後房貸要背二三十年，以後也沒有閒錢出國去玩，我還是決定再緩一緩。畢竟我現在也還住家裡，不需要房子。

決定四 | 投資理財 Investment

我看朋友投資股市還做得不錯，常常都有賺錢。我也在想是不要要拿點錢出來投資，可是我又不懂股票市場，萬一賠光了我又要從頭開始，不如我請朋友操盤，給她賺點傭金。是有點風險可是我目前還有小賺一點。我覺得有時候就是要放手一搏。

決定五 | 分手 The break up

我真的很愛我的前男友，可是我抓到他外面有小三，雖然他打死不承認，可是我知道他不忠是事實。我實在過不了自己這關，我就算跟他分手我還是會很想他，所以我決定睜一隻眼閉一隻眼。可是到最後那個女的有了，我也不得不跟他分手。

決定六｜結婚 Marriage

跟女朋友交往五年了，去年她一直催我結婚，其實我也是很想娶她但是我一直覺得我的工作向來不穩定，養家是很大的責任。她一直說她年紀到了，不趕快生她會變成高齡產婦。我爸媽也覺得早點定下來是好事，我們就決定結婚了，目前我覺得還習慣這種生活。

決定七｜辭職 Resignation

大學畢業後好不容易找到一份工作，雖然不是理想的工作，但是至少有一份穩定的薪水。不過我一直覺得同事在找我麻煩，老是嫌東嫌西。還在老闆面前說我不好。我撐了三個月到最後還是決定辭職，因為做自己不喜歡的工作真的是度日如年。

決定八｜北上找工作 Heading north

碩士畢業之後我想趟台北闖闖，雖然人生地不熟，但是還是去。沒想到我的際遇還不錯，遇到個願意給我機會的老闆。雖然薪水並不高，再加上房租生活費，實在沒剩什麼錢。做了幾年決定回南部來，有台北的工作經驗回到南部倒是很實用。

Q4 Please describe an important decision in your life.

MP3 40

請描述一個你人生中重要的決定

念哪個科系 Choosing major

I had a hard time making the decision about the major I'm going to take, knowing it would have a major impact on my career life in the future.

選科系的時候我實在很難下決定，因為我知道這會影響我未來工作的方向。

I always like dancing and I always dream to be a professional dancer one day I have been taking dance classes since I was little, and I was pretty talented, too.

我一直都很喜歡跳舞，也想像有一天可以當個專業舞者，我從小就學舞，而且也蠻有天份的。

But when I start to look at the reality, I am not confident that I can make a living as a dancer. I know I am a good dancer and with more training, I will be an outstanding one !

可是當我想到實際面的時候，我實在沒把握當舞者可以填飽肚子。我知道我跳得很好，如果透過適當的訓練我會變得更傑出。

However, I think the reality of being a part of the entertainment business is pretty cruel. I am not the tallest or the finest looking dancer on the dance floor. I guess it kind of limited my opportunities.

可是娛樂業的現實面是很殘忍的，放眼看過去我也不是最高挑最漂亮的舞者，我看我還是算了。

It was a painful decision, but I decided to do commerce instead. I think commerce would fit in this society better, and I also believe the salary of business related position would be able to support the lifestyle I want. I gave in to reality !

下這個決定實在很痛苦，可是我決定要念商科。因為商科的性質比較容易被這個社會接受。而且我也相信從商的薪水可以達到我想要的生活型態。

I don't mind being in the accounting firm, and I don't regret what I chose. But somehow I always wonder, if I ever did take up dancing, where would I be today？ Maybe I would be performing in Broadway or being part of a

我不介意現在在會計公司的職務，我也不後悔我的選擇，可是我偶而會幻想如果我當初選擇舞蹈系的話，現在會在哪裡？ 我可能會在百

dancing company touring the world！ You just never know！

老匯表演，搞不好會跟知名舞團去世界巡迴表演！ 真的很難說呢！

音樂

請描述你喜歡聽的音樂類型

音樂一｜交響樂 Symphony Orchestra

我很喜歡去音樂廳看交響樂團的演出，我覺得欣賞現場的音樂演奏表演很有震撼力。有些人可能會覺得交響樂很無聊，可是我覺得聽交響樂讓我的思路更清晰，我喜歡閉上眼睛仔細地聆聽旋律的起伏，陶醉在大提琴的低沉的音符裡。

音樂二｜沙發音樂 Lounge music

我最喜歡沙發音樂，尤其是咖啡廳裡播放的沙發音樂，不知道是不是裝潢的關係，在那裡聽沙發音樂真的很舒服。我覺得沙發音樂讓人很放鬆，雖然沒有很強的節奏感，但是輕快的旋律讓我會不自主地跟著哼唱，一邊看雜誌一邊聽音樂真是享受。

音樂三｜雷鬼音樂 Reggae

我喜歡聽雷鬼音樂因為我不知不覺地就會融入音樂跟著搖擺。尤其是工作壓力大想去度假的時候。我總是想像著手上拿了杯調酒，靠在海灘上的露天酒吧旁邊，望著藍天碧海，還有沙灘上滿滿的比基尼辣妹，頓時心情好很多。

音樂四｜爵士樂 Jazz

幾年前到紐約找高中同學，他帶我到爵士樂酒吧聽歌。我從此之後就愛上爵士樂那種時而輕快又時而浪漫的節奏。爵士酒吧的氣氛很好，通常並不太大，聽眾跟樂團的距離很近，你可以清楚地感受到演奏者的情緒，很有震撼力。

音樂五｜英文經典情歌 English classic love songs

我從小就喜歡聽英文經典情歌，一開始是因為英文情歌很受歡迎，到處都聽得到，也因為常聽到，所以非常想學會歌詞跟著唱。我買了很多 CD，常常一邊聽一邊看著歌詞學唱，唱多了也開始了解歌詞的意義，因此我還學了不少片語呢。

音樂六｜國語流行歌曲 Chinese pop music

我最喜歡聽國語流行歌了，像周杰倫，蔡依林之類能歌善舞的主流派。無論是節奏強烈的舞曲或是帶點傷感的情歌，我都不排斥。我想是因為中文歌的關係，我可以很清楚地了解歌詞想表達的意義，很容易就可以融入歌曲的意境。

音樂七｜嘻哈舞曲 Hip Hop

可能是因為看舞力全開系列電影的影響，我好喜歡聽嘻哈舞曲。我是沒辦法像專業舞者那樣靈活，但是我至少還可以隨著音樂點頭搖擺，看起來也蠻有感覺的。我覺得嘻哈舞曲很有活力，節奏很強烈，一邊開車一邊大聲聽就像美國的黑幫！

音樂八｜拉丁情歌 Latino love songs

我不懂西班牙文，可是我深深的被拉丁情歌吸引。有的是電影的配樂，有的是舞蹈的背景音樂。雖然我不懂歌詞在唱什麼，可是從旋律還有音調中，可以清楚地感覺到演唱者的熱情，很有異國風的感覺，真想站起來一起扭腰擺臀！

Q5 What music do you like to listen to?

MP3 41

請描述你喜歡聽的音樂類型

韓國流行音樂 K Pop

My favourite music would be K Pop. I think they have the best boy bands and girl bands in the world! Their songs are really catchy. You don't have to know Korean to know how to sing along for a few sentences, like "Gang-nam style" by Psy and "No body" by Wonder girls.

我最喜歡的音樂就是韓國流行音樂，我覺得他們的男子和女子樂團真是世界第一！他們的歌曲很容易琅琅上口，就算你不會韓文也可以跟著唱幾句，就像江南大叔的 Gangnam style 還有 Wonder girls 唱的 No-body。

I once watched this documentary about the inside of forming a Korean pop band. Not only do they want the band to be popular in Korea, their ultimate goal is to

我曾經看過一段有關韓國團體的秘辛，他們的目標不只是要在韓國成功，最終目標是要把韓國流

make Korean Pop music an international success.

行音樂推向世界。

To achieve that, the record companies have to make sure they have got the best cards in hand. Apparently, every single component is carefully thought out and executed, when it comes to a team member selection, training and most importantly, the song selection.

為了要達成這個目標，唱片公司必須要好好計畫，並確認每個步驟都做得正確。尤其是選擇團員，嚴格的訓練還有最重要的是歌曲的選擇。

How to make people who do not understand Korean to like Korean songs is one big challenge, if you pay attention to those popular Korean songs, you will notice they all have part of it in English.

要如何讓不懂韓文的人唱韓國歌曲可是個大挑戰，如果你仔細聽，你會發現他們的歌裡面都一定會有一段英文。

Apparently, hundreds of songs are discarded for every one song that is selected. This is how much effort they put in to make sure the song is right.

而且他們是從幾百首歌中挑出一首歌，這就是他們對歌曲選擇的用心。

I think K Pop is the whole package, the team members are expected to look a certain way too. So many fans are willing to go under the knife just to enhance their look to look more like their favourite pop star. I must say K pop does wonders to people !

我覺得 K Pop 是一種文化，所有的團員看起來都有種特定的樣子，讓很多歌迷更是不顧一切的去動刀，就為了讓自己看起來像喜歡的歌手。我只能說韓國天團還有讓人變美的神奇力量呢！

國家

請描述一個你想去的國家，還有為什麼想去？

國家一｜英國 UK

我最想去的國家是英國，我很想去那裡讀書。我選擇英國是因為英國是個很有文化氣息的國家，更是英語的發源地，我想去學正統的英語，希望有幸能見到英國女皇。我也想去體驗看看英國的男孩是不是真的比較紳士，最好每個都像貝克漢！

國家二｜法國 France

那一定是法國了，我從小就幻想在艾菲爾鐵塔拍婚紗，那有多浪漫啊！ 再加上法國的街景，浪漫的情侶，街邊的露天咖啡廳。還有普羅旺斯的薰衣草田，再來杯法國香檳就更完美了！可是近年來法國的恐怖攻擊不斷，真讓我有點擔心。

國家三 | 義大利 Italy

我最想去看威尼斯水都的真面目，在旅遊節目上常看到遊客搭著鳳尾船穿梭在威尼斯的運河裡。就連 007 的電影都曾在那裏取景，威尼斯一定有與眾不同的地方。到了義大利一定要嘗一下正宗的披薩還有義大利麵，比較一下跟台灣的口味有什麼不同。

國家四 | 帛琉 Palau

我最喜歡去海島國家玩，享受陽光沙灘的度假感覺，我超愛浮潛的！帛琉群島有個特別的水母湖，湖裡面的水母全都沒有毒性，不會螫人。有多少人能說他們很享受跟水母一起游泳的感覺呢？ 大部分的人游泳遇到水母只會想逃跑吧！

國家五 | 日本 Japan

我最想去日本，因為離台灣很近，三個小時的飛機就到了。雖然語言不通可是因為他們用的漢字很多，用猜的意思上也差不多。還有我超迷日本的動漫，櫻花妹們又最愛玩 Cosplay，每個打扮起來都很迷人，希望她們會想要跟我交朋友。

國家六｜阿拉伯聯合大公國 United Arab Emirates (UAE)

我一直都想到中東國家去看看，可是不太敢去，因為對回教國家實在不太熟悉，我很擔心會不小心侵犯到他們的教義。可是杜拜應該算是中東最西化的城市了，我好想去體驗所謂六星級的帆船飯店是怎樣的規格，他們的摩天大樓也破了台北 101 的紀錄。

國家七｜祕魯 Peru

我喜歡去神秘古老的國家看古蹟，祕魯最吸引我的地方就是天空之城-馬丘比丘。我去過柬埔寨看吳哥窟，我覺得很雄偉，可是朋友告訴我馬丘比丘比吳哥窟更加令人嘆為觀止。我還要趁年輕體力好才能去，因為馬丘比丘在很高的山上。

國家八｜美國 United States of America (USA)

美國是我最嚮往的國家，我們從小到大所受的教育、資訊都是深深受美國影響。電視電影更不用說，我真的好想一睹紐約中央公園的風采，還有大峽谷的鬼斧神工，拉斯維加斯的不夜城。我最希望可以走在街上跟明星不期而遇！

Q6 Please tell me a country you would like to visit, and why？

MP3 42

請描述一個你想去的國家，還有為什麼想去？

澳洲 Australia

I would love to visit Australia, maybe move there for a bit to do working holidays. I was told if you tried hard enough, you could really save a lot of money within a year.

我會很想去澳洲，可以的話去當背包客一陣子也不錯。我聽說如果你努力一點的話，你一年之內就可以存不少錢。

I have been planning for it since I graduated from university. But I haven't quite worked up the courage to go over on my own yet. I would prefer to travel with a partner, so we can look out for each other, but so far I still haven't found someone who would like to go together.

我從大學畢業就開始有這個想法，可是我一直還沒有勇氣自己去。我會希望有同伴可以一起去，大家互相照顧，可是到現在我還沒找到志同道合的人。

Australia is a big country compared with Taiwan. Most of its' population and attractions are in the east coast. Some of the famous attractions are: Uluru, Sydney opera house, Gold Coast, and so on.

跟台灣比起來的話，澳洲是個大國。大部分的人口和觀光勝地都在東岸，知名景點有:艾爾斯岩，雪梨歌劇院，黃金海岸等等。

And what I want to do the most is to take a diving tour in the world famous Great Barrier Reef. I heard so much about it, apparently you can join this tour which takes you out diving for a day to a few famous spots and you might get to swim alongside this friendly fish called Big Willy.

而我最想要做的事就是到大堡礁潛水，我聽了很多有關大堡礁的事，在那裡你可參加潛水一日遊。他們會帶你到幾個潛水的景點，如果運氣好的話還可能遇到一隻叫大威利的魚，他會游過來跟你玩。

I am also very interested in all the native animals there, such as Kangaroos, Koalas, and wombats. I was told it is likely to see Kangaroos in the wild especially

我也很想去看當地的動物，就像袋鼠、無尾熊，還有袋熊。我聽說在郊外常常可以看到野生袋

during dusk when they are out looking for food. That is just something you need to go to experience yourself.

鼠，尤其是傍晚他們出來覓食的時候，我覺得這真的是要自己來體驗才會了解那種感覺。

I am not sure whether my trip would eventually happen because you have to go before you turn 30, and the time is ticking.

我不知道我到底會不會去，因為條件是你三十歲生日前要出發，我也快三十了。

廣告

請描述一段你覺得有趣的廣告

廣告一｜樂透彩券 Lottery

一對看起來很窮的父子在火車上，兒子看著沿途的風景，不斷地告訴爸爸他看到了什麼東西，例如說：房子跟汽車等等。爸爸就會反問他喜歡嗎？ 兒子就點點頭，爸爸手上拿著他剛買的樂透彩券，一邊笑著幻想著中獎之後他會有很多錢，他不停地跟兒子說，爸爸買給你！ 一券在手，希望無窮。

廣告二｜汽車廣告 Peugeot

一個印度型男因為嫌他的車款太舊，又負擔不起新車，所以他突發奇想，決定把舊車的外型用各種方式，例如向前撞牆把引擎撞凹，望後倒車把原本的防車撞成掀背車的後車外型。加上其他的敲敲打打，終於把他的舊車重新塑形為 Peugeot 的新車款，他很驕傲地開出去把妹。

廣告三｜蠻牛廣告 Taiwanese Red bull

一個很瘦小的老公不斷地為了討好肥老婆而盡力去達成她的要求，一下要煮飯，一下要上班、一下要接小孩，還要幫老婆全身按摩，最後在他上氣不接下氣喘息的時候，背景聲音問他，你累了嗎？ 他喝了提神飲料之後，立刻精神百倍。

廣告四｜報紙的贈品廣告 Newspaper

一個上班族正要準備早餐，把土司放進烤麵包機，打開瓦斯爐準備煎個蛋，低低下頭去看吐司烤好了沒有，沒想到吐司正好烤好跳起來打到他的眼睛，他不自主的轉身想扶住流理台，沒想到去是把手放到燒熱的鍋子上，此時出現訂報紙就送急救包的標語。

廣告五｜海尼根 Heineke

一個美女正要伸手去拿在架子最高處的啤酒，卻一直搆不到。此時來了一個男客人也剛好要去拿同一瓶啤酒，美女想說這個男的會展現紳士風度拿下來給她，沒想到只剩最後一瓶了，那個男的就拿走趕快轉身去付帳！ 美女就一臉驚訝。

廣告六｜福斯汽車 Volkswagen

廣告裡有一隻小狗用嘴叼起狗鍊要主人帶牠去散步，主人一臉無奈的帶牠出門，因為主人知道散步時狗的行為會讓人看傻眼。小狗一邊跑一邊模仿汽車的聲音，會有加速的引擎聲，轉彎還有甩尾聲，倒退還會學倒車雷達，停下來還有防盜器的聲音。當鄰居開著福斯的車款回來，小狗興奮到好像看到同類！

廣告七｜電話簿付費廣告 Yellow pages

有一個在海生館工作的清潔工一邊跳舞一邊打掃，結果拖把柄不小心把鯊魚區圍欄的玻璃撞裂了一角，玻璃開始慢慢裂開，他一邊用手擋住裂縫不要讓玻璃爆開，一邊等著他的同伴拿出傳統的電話簿開始找維修玻璃的廠商，眼看鯊魚就要把玻璃撞破了，此時就跳出電話簿刊登廣告的服務專線。

廣告八｜貸款公司 Mortgage broker

一位爸爸好意去接女兒還有女兒的朋友們從派對回家，大家都喝多了在車上高歌歡唱，途中女兒的朋友們說要停車一下，去超商買個東西，大家都下車了爸爸把女兒叫回來要，女兒靠在車窗旁爸爸掏出錢拿給她，此時警察出現了，因為這個景象看起來很像男人在路邊召妓。主要是廣告一家貸款銀行不會不問清楚就不貸款給你。

Q7 Please describe a TV commercial that you think it is interesting.

MP3 43

請描述一段你覺得有趣的廣告

眼鏡公司廣告 SpecSaver

This commercial is created for a glasses company called SpecSaver in Australia. They are aiming to differentiate themselves for being more affordable than the others.

這個廣告是澳洲一家叫 SpecSaver 眼鏡公司的電視廣告。他們的訴求就是要以價格將他們與其他競爭者區隔開來。

One day, a son came to his elderly mother's house to visit her, and they are having tea and cake in the kitchen with the view of her garden. He noticed that she was wearing a new pair of glasses. He commented on how nice those glasses are, and it must have costed her a lot of money.

有一天兒子回家看媽媽，跟媽媽在廚房喝下午茶一邊聊天，他家的廚房看出去就是花園。他注意到他媽媽配了一副新的眼鏡，他稱讚那副眼鏡很好看，一定很貴吧！

She then replied and said, No, the insurance would cover it. Then the son started to question how expensive the lenses must be. She replied: It is 25% off on all lenses. I went to SpecSaver and don't you worry I am not spending your inheritance.

他媽媽回答：沒有，保險都有給付。兒子又說：那鏡片也一定要不少錢吧？媽媽回答：鏡片也都有打七五折，放心啦兒子，我不會隨便把你的遺產給花掉，我是去 SpecSaver 配的！

The son acted relaxed and said to her, Good！ Then his mother said something that makes him really worried. She looked through the window and said to him: Don't you worry, I am leaving them all to Dereck. He turned his head then saw this hot, sexy and topless guy trimming the trees for his mother. The look on his face is priceless！ He was in such shock.

兒子聽了就放心地說，那很好！結果沒想到他媽媽說你別擔心，我全部都要留給德瑞克！兒子轉頭順著他媽媽的視線看過去，沒想到看到一個沒穿上衣的性感猛男正在幫他媽修剪花園裡的樹枝。他真的臉都綠了！完全嚇傻了！

I think this commercial is simple but clever. The ending caught everyone by surprise. Viewers get the idea how competitive their price is straight away, but at the same time the commercial does not make the SpecSaver seems like a cheap place. It still looks quite classy. I think that is why this commercial left an impression.

我覺得這個廣告拍得很淺顯易懂，結尾更是在大家的意料之外。觀眾看完就知道他們眼鏡的價錢很有競爭力，而且同時也不覺得 SpecSaver 是一間很廉價的公司，還是蠻有品味的。這應該是我對這個廣告印象深刻的原因。

幫助

請描述一段你曾經幫助別人的經驗

經驗一｜喜憨兒基金會 Children Are Us foundation

每年母親節喜憨兒基金會的糕餅工廠都會推出送愛到部落的活動，除了訂一份給我媽媽之外，我都會多一份送給偏鄉部落的弱勢家庭。一方面是增加喜憨兒工廠的收入還有工作機會，另一方面是弱勢家庭也可以享受節慶的感覺，知道有人祝福著他們。

經驗二｜幫忙募款 Fundraising

莫拉克風災的時候雖然是台灣很痛苦的時期，但也感受到台灣的上下一心，真是有錢出錢，有力出力。我沒有辦法到南部災區去幫忙，所以我能做的就是幫忙募款。連續幾個禮拜我都跟著紅十字會的人拿著捐款箱到處去募款，我覺得很有意義。

經驗三｜請人讓座給孕婦 Priority seat

我高中時候需要坐公車上、下課，有一次剛好有位孕婦上車，她手上還提著不少東西，車上人很多，前排位子的人睡著了，我趕緊跟叫醒他，請他讓座給孕婦。雖然不是我直接讓位給孕婦，但是我覺得我也是做了件好事，她很感謝我。

經驗四｜撿到手機歸還 Return the cellphone

有一次在提款機旁邊撿到一隻手機，我並沒有看到有人在我前面剛領完錢，所以我猜他可能剛走。我也有事不能在原地等，所以我拿他的手機查一下他通訊錄，他有存家裡的電話，我就打過去跟她家人說我撿到他的手機，並留下我的電話跟她約時間把手機拿回去。

經驗五｜當義工 Volunteering

我媽是廟裡的信徒，有一次廟裡想要回饋鄉里，想把供品捐給孤兒院，但是找不到人可以送過去。我就自願當義工，跟我老爸借車，還自掏腰包多買了一些小孩子喜歡的禮物，一併帶過去。院長對於外來的捐助都很感謝。我假日也偶而會過去看看有什麼可以幫忙的。

經驗六｜參加淨灘活動 Clean the beach campaign

我在網路上看到有個外國人在台灣發起淨灘活動，我在想我自己是台灣人，我怎麼能不愛護這片土地。所以我就跟著到福隆淨灘，其中不乏外國人，可是大部分都是台灣人，我很高興能為這片土地盡一點心力，也因此認識了很多跟我有相同想法的新朋友。

經驗七｜叫人起床 Wake up call

有一次坐高鐵回台北，坐我旁邊的是個有點年紀的媽媽。她上車時打了通電話，我聽她的口氣應該是要在台中下車，講完電話她也就睡著了。車一路開，很快的廣播就說台中站到了。我看她還在睡，我就推一推她，跟她說台中到了，她馬上從座位上跳起來拿起包包就衝出去！

經驗八｜機車意外 Scooter accident

有一次我走在馬路旁的人行道上，剛好經過路口所有的車停下來等紅燈。突然間有一台最靠近路邊的機車連人帶車倒下來，剛好就離我兩三步的距離，我趕快幫忙把車扶起來，還好那個機車騎士沒受傷，他沒注意到旁邊是排水孔，一腳踩空。

Please describe a situation when you helped someone.

請描述一段你曾經幫助別人的經驗

世界展望會 World vision

Ever since I got my first stable job, I said to myself that I want to do something for someone and pay it forward. I happened to see the campaign for World Vision and how they help out poor kids around the world. I decided to sign up with them as a sponsor. It does not cost much, only 7 hundred dollars a month, and it can change somcone else's life completely. I think I can afford that !

自從我有第一份穩定的工作開始，我就跟我自己說要做些有意義可以回饋社會的事。我剛好看到世界展望會的幫助世界貧童的廣告，所以決定加入成為資助人。一個月才台幣 700 元就可以完全改變另一個人的生活，那我真的花得起這個錢。

The kid that was assigned to me is a 5 years old boy from Kenya. His name is Aton, and he has

我分到的兒童是一位五歲的非洲肯亞男童，他叫做阿堂，

5 other siblings. His parents do simple farming trying to support the family but with the weather conditions, what they get in return is not very much, and is totally not sustainable.

他的家有其他五個兄弟姊妹。他爸媽只能種植一點簡單的東西來維生，可是因為氣候的關係收成很差，根本不可靠。

With my sponsorship, not only does Aton get the education that he needs, but also there will be regular food hamper delivered to his family. I think I help more than just one person.

因為有我的資助金，阿堂不只可以去上學，他們家也固定會收到糧食包。我覺得受惠的不只是他而已。

I have been doing it for over 10 years now, and I don't think I would ever stop being a sponsor. I was just wondering what happens once Aton turns 18, does that mean he wouldn't need the sponsorship anymore？ I guess they might give me another kid to sponsor since there are so many kids in need especially in the third

我已經資助他十年了，我覺得我會一直資助下去。我只是在想如果等阿堂滿 18 歲之後，展望會就不再資助他嗎？我猜他們應該會分另一個小孩給我吧，畢竟在第三世界國家需要資助的小孩是數以

world countries. I really think it is meaningful to be a sponsor like that. I hope there will be more people feel the same.

萬計。我覺得當資助人是很有意義的事，我希望會有越來越多的人跟我有同感。

汙染

請描述一項你目前居住地區可能或是正面臨的汙染問題

汙染一｜水汙染 Water pollution

台灣的水汙染很嚴重，特別是不肖工廠偷排放廢水的問題，不但造成下游農地汙染，還有河川生態的汙染。高雄的後勁溪就常常發現有人偷排廢水，不但溪裡充滿了死魚蝦，甚至整條河都變了顏色，很難想像有多少毒素進排了水裡。

污染二｜土地汙染 Soil pollution

高雄的中油煉油廠終於在 2015 年關閉了，可是在過去 25 年裡，對於土地的污染早已造成。附近的土地根本不適合栽種農產品，甚至連地下水也不能使用。聽說要整治需要長達 20 年的時間，而且需要大筆經費。也不知道政府是否真的有計畫要處理這個問題。

污染三｜光害汙染 Light pollution

我在台北租的房子是在透天厝的二樓，窗口正是樓下美式酒吧的招牌，每天晚上霓虹燈閃個不停，要到十二點他們才打烊，我想早點睡都不行，因為就算我買了遮光窗簾，它還是會透光。再加上街邊的 LED 路燈直接射進我的窗口，光害真的很嚴重。

汙染四｜噪音汙染 Noise pollution

我家剛好在台南最出名的花園夜市附近，一到晚上就塞車，根本找不到停車位。人潮聲車流聲不斷，再加上發電機轟轟作響的聲音，每天至少吵到半夜。我想全台灣住在夜市附近的居民了解我這種痛苦，可是好像也沒有什麼法規可以規範。

汙染四｜空氣汙染 Air pollution

説到空氣汙染，台灣真是腹背受敵。除了國內工廠自己產生的廢氣汙染，還要擔心對岸中國飄過來的廢氣、沙塵暴之類的。這種看不見的 PM2.5 對人體的影響遠超過我們想像，也因為看不見，我們常常掉以輕心。我現在出門都會乖乖戴口罩。

汙染五｜垃圾汙染 Solid waste pollution

雖然在台灣老早就已經實施垃圾不落地的政策，對外國人來，說看台灣人追垃圾車真是一種奇觀。可是在我老家彰化，還是會有人習慣在電線桿亂丟垃圾，很多東西都是可以回收再利用的。我覺得可能還是需要多宣導，不然鄉下還是看起又髒又亂。

汙染六｜外來物種汙染 Invasive species pollution

現在進口的農產品很多，雖然政府一定會有適當的檢測，可是因為是農產品，很難保證沒有外來的小蟲躲在裡面。外來物種對原生的動植物都有一定的威脅。現在交通這麼方便，難保不會有茲卡病毒的蚊子搭著飛機從南美洲到台灣，只是時間的問題。

汙染七｜視覺汙染 Visual pollution

開在高速公路上大家都想看到鄉村的美景，或是日落海邊閃耀的餘暉，可是偏偏高速公路的兩旁卻是廣告牌林立。有賣房子的、借錢的、抓姦的，實在讓人感覺很不好。為什麼不能像國外一樣就只有美景，我覺得如果台灣可以改善這種視覺汙染，我們的觀光產業應該會更好。

Q9 Please describe a pollution you are facing or might be facing in your area.

MP3 45

請描述一項你目前居住地區可能或是正面臨的汙染問題

輻射汙染 Radioactive pollution

I never used to think radioactive pollution could affect our life so much. It was a foreign concept to me until the Tsunami hit Japan a few years back which damaged a nuclear power plant in Fukushima, and caused the radiation to leak out.

我以前從來不覺得輻射污染會對我們的生活帶來這麼大的影響，一直到幾年前日本海嘯使福島核電廠受損，造成輻射外洩之前，輻射污染對我來說是一個很陌生的名詞。

Japanese fresh produce was one of the top shell items you can get in the market, and people were willing to pay top dollar for. I personally love their apples and seafood, but I haven't been buy-

從前，日本的農產品是市場上最高等級的東西，大家都願意花大錢去買。我最喜歡他們的蘋果還有海鮮了，可是自從海

ing them for a long time since the disaster happened. I am really wary about the residue from the radiation although all exporters claimed they have passed the radiation check and quality controls.

嘯之後我已經很久沒買了，因為我很擔心輻射的殘留。雖然出口商都保證他們的產品都有通過輻射還有品質的檢測。

But no one can guarantee that it is 100 percent safe to eat. Maybe you would not see the effect until later in your life. As much as I love the produce, I decided to seek for alternatives.

可是沒有人敢保證百分百的安全，可能要很久以後才看的到結果。雖然我真的很愛吃，可是我還是決定找其他替代產品。

Being so close to Japan, I don't even know whether our seafood is radiation free because some of the species would travel to Taiwanese water through currents.

我們離日本這麼近，我也不敢確定我們的海鮮沒有輻射汙染，因為有些魚種是會透過洋流到台灣海域的！

This really makes me think twice about opening up more nu-

這不禁讓我想到台灣核電廠的安全，

clear power plants in Taiwan. If we have a disaster occurring in a high population density area, one could escape from it. The direct contact with the radiation would make us sick, too. Maybe we need to seek for alternative energy sources.

如果這種災害發生在台灣人口稠密的地區，那可是會無一倖免的！ 直接受到輻射的接觸可是會讓人生病的，可能尋找替代能源會比較好。

國家的問題

請描述一項目前你的國家可能面臨的問題

問題一｜社會福利問題 Social welfare

前幾年搞得大家人心惶惶，勞保到底還要不要保，退休金該怎麼領，沒有人有個正確答案，只能祈禱勞保不要倒。健保保費常常調漲，保障的項目卻不見得更完善。退休如果只靠國民年金的話，根本就不夠用。政府真的需要有好一點的配套措施。

問題二｜食安問題 Food safety

本來我對台灣製造的食品很有信心，對我來說，那些黑心食品都是大陸或是其他第三世界國家才會有的問題，結果沒想到連我們從小吃到大的食品都是問題食品，而且還是那些所謂的優良廠商，我們真的無所適從。政府真的監督得不嚴格。

問題三｜教育問題 Education

台灣的教育制度近年來不斷地改來改去，因為我自己沒有小孩所以我已經不了瞭解目前最新的制度是什麼了！ 一下是 12 年國教，一下又是學測，所謂的聯考老早就已經廢掉了。各個學校一綱多本，我只能用一個亂字來形容，都把大家當白老鼠。

問題四｜低薪問題 Low average income

我最氣政府說低薪是國家的競爭力，我覺得這句話根本就是看不起台灣年輕人的創意還有理想的價值。 所以年輕人畢業後找不到可以養家活口的工作，情願到澳洲打工當背包客，雖然是做粗活，可是一兩年下來可以存到的錢卻是在台灣一般上班族做不到的。

問題五｜房價問題 Housing affordability

房價居高不下，無論政府端出什麼打房的政策，好像成效都不彰。因為城鄉差距，在人口密集的大都市裡，年輕人是買不起房子的，就連租金也貴得嚇人。國宅的數量也不夠，難怪結婚生小孩的人口越來越少，想要有個自己的家還真難。

問題六｜治安問題 Crime and safety

近年來隨機殺人或傷人的事件不斷發生，犯案內容的驚悚程度頻頻登上國際媒體。我不知道應該怎麼預防這種隨機的事件，也許我們需要更多警力來巡視，或是從基本開始關心弱勢家庭或是暴力家庭。總不能每次都怪運氣不好遇上這種事。

問題七｜國安問題 Boarder security

其他國家的人不能明白台灣人的處境，在國際上不被其他國家認同是一件很心酸的事。我們的漁船一天到晚被其他國家扣押，海外犯罪的台灣人被送往大陸處置，國際賽事還只能自稱中華台北，我看也只有巴勒斯坦人才會懂我們的感受。

問題八｜天然災害問題 Nature disaster

台灣的天然災害還真不少，常常是颱風帶來驚人的雨量把整個山區村落移為平地，可是同一個時間平地卻無水可用鬧旱災。七八月份停水是很可怕的，每個人都汗流浹背怎麼能不洗澡。我覺得政府應該投入研究其他開發水資源的方式，這樣可以避免缺水的窘境。

Q10 Please describe a possible problem in your country might be facing.

MP3 46

請描述一項目前你的國家可能面臨的問題

詐騙集團問題 Scam syndicate

For some reason scam syndicates are everywhere in Taiwan. I would say almost every single one of us would have an encounter with them at one point or another. It is so common that the government would advertise on TV to warn people to not believe what people told you over phone easily.

不知道為什麼在台灣詐騙集團真的很猖獗，我敢說幾乎每一個人都有遇過。就連政府都意識到要在電視上宣導不要輕易地相信電話中的人。

The thing is, they sound so convincing, even when they are pretending they work for tax office or other government departments. They are very professional and

事實是，詐騙集團都很能言善道，就連裝成政府部門的員工都那麼的專業，訓練有素。我記得有一

well trained. I remember one time I received this call to notify me that I won a big lump sum of money but in order to claim the money, I have to first transfer them the 20% tax.

次我接到電話說我中獎得了一大筆錢，可是要先匯百分之 20 的稅金給他們才可以把獎金給我。

I knew immediately it is a scam, and I didn't fall for it. However, there are still people falling for the traps and losing their life savings.

這一聽就知道是詐騙，我才沒有上當呢！可是還是有很多人連畢生積蓄都被騙光了。

A lot of scam syndicates have their headquarters based overseas to avoid police investigation. In some cases, the police are able to catch the scapegoat of the syndicate, which is the person who is hired by the syndicate to collect the money in public. However, it is difficult to bring the chief of the syndicate to justice because they are always behind the scenes. I must give the police

很多詐騙集團的總部都設在海外以逃避偵查。有時候警方抓到的只是代罪羔羊，不過是集團聘僱的車手，負責出面領錢而已。很難將集團的首腦定罪因為他們都藏在幕後。但我也必須要給警方一點讚賞，因為不久前他們偵破一個國際犯罪集

some credit because not long ago they busted an international scam syndicate who was scamming bank ATM system in Taiwan. I was very impressed they not only caught some of the people but also retrieved most of the money which is unheard of !

團專門在台灣破解銀行的提款機系統，他們不但抓到幾個人，居然還有辦法把部分的錢追回來，實在太猛了！

書籍

請描述一本你喜歡的書籍或是雜誌

書籍一｜哈利波特 Harry Potter

雖然很多人覺得哈利波特是給小孩子看的，可是我覺得哈利波特的情節很引人入勝。故事內容主要是說哈利波特從小被阿姨一家人當成怪胎，直到他被帶入充滿魔法還有想像力的神奇世界，一連串的冒險情節，也解開了他的身世之謎。

書籍二｜賈伯斯傳 Steve Jobs by Walton Isaacson

大家都知道一手創造蘋果的賈伯斯，這本賈伯斯傳不單單只是談論賈伯斯的一生，更是藉由它來談創新的概念。賈伯斯和蘋果的員工不只有理念，更是精益求精，嚴格控制品管，充分結合想像力和極致的工藝科技。我覺得很有啟發性。

書籍三｜富爸爸窮爸爸 Rich dad Poor dad by Robert T. Kiyosaki

這是一本財經書籍，但是他講的財經觀念，並不像一般高談闊論的財經書教你如何投資理財。作者用他本身的故事，他與他爸爸之間的互動來推翻找個穩定工作過一輩子的觀念。我覺得對即將出社會的學子們很有幫助，讓他們用不同的角度看賺錢這回事。

書籍四｜行銷妙招 Sales psychology by Fong Sheng Lee

我本身是做業務的，所以跟客戶的溝通接洽很重要，我從這本書中學到很多話術還有推敲客戶心思的技巧。也發現我以前的方式不太有效率是因為我沒有找對方法。作者用平易近人的白話方式來寫作，我覺得很容易閱讀，收穫很大。

書籍五｜印度廚房 World kitchen - Indian published by Murdoch books

我很喜歡吃印度菜，可是在台灣印度餐廳並不普遍，而且價格也高，我決定買食譜自己做做看。書裡面除了食譜之外，還有教很多做印度烤餅的技法及秘訣。從中我也認識到很多我們不熟悉的香料種類以及如何應用香料。我試過幾次都蠻成功的。

書籍六｜壹週刊 Next Magazine (Tabloid)

我平時對讀書沒什麼興趣，偶而喜歡看看八卦雜誌，而最好看的就是壹週刊。他們的標題都很聳動，內文的陳述也很詳細，雖然有時候有點粗俗，但是卻形容得很貼切。配上狗仔偷拍的照片，讀起來根本不用花腦筋去想，很放鬆。

書籍七｜第一次自助旅行就上手 Self-guided travel for first timers by Lin & Kuo

我以前出國都是跟團，很想嘗試自助旅行可是又有點害怕，看了這本書之後我覺得自助旅行沒那麼可怕，只要把主要的行程規劃好，有點小狀況也不用太擔心。而且書裡面也有很多求助的電話和方式，希望我用不上，可是有資料在手總是比較心安。

書籍八｜面對父母老去的勇氣 How to care for your parents when they are aging by Ichiro Kishimi

這本書帶給我很大的感動，作者是在教所有做人子女的應該如何換個方式跟年紀越來越大的父母相處，尤其是父母年紀大變得越來越嘮叨，越來越固執或是身體有病痛。學校只有教我們要孝順父母，但卻沒有教我們如何與他們相處，看完之後我有很多新的體會。

Q11 Please tell me about a book or a magazine you like.

MP3 47

請描述一本你喜歡的書籍或是雜誌

人生不設限 Life without limits by Nick Vujicic

Speaking of Nick Vujicic who is the author of this book, I believe most of us have heard about him. He was born without limbs which is a rare form of disability. The book " Life without limits" is a reflection on his life, you can imagine being born with such a severe deformity, his life would not be smooth.

說到這本書的作者力克胡哲，應該沒有人不認識，他出生就沒有四肢，是一種罕見的病例。人生不設限這本書是他人生的回顧，可以想見他一生下來就有這麼嚴重的缺陷，他的人生一定充滿挫折。

I am not surprised he did attempt to end his life a few times since he was still a child. I feel really bad for him being forced to deal with teasing and scorn and bullied so badly at school, I mean

聽到他說小時候就有好幾次試著結束自己的生命，其實我並不驚訝。我覺得很難過他求學過程中被迫面對了多少輕蔑苛

I am a normal kid but I still get teased about being fat or ugly. You know what kids are like at school.

薄的言語還有欺負他的人。你也知道小孩就是這樣，我算是個正常人，都會有人說我肥或是醜了，何況是他。

It does take him quite some time to realize that he needs to change his attitude if he still wants to live and he needs to turn his life around. My favorite quote in the book is: “Life without limbs or life without limits” and he did just that！ He knows he can’t sit around to wait for the miracle to happen for him, or he needs to turn himself into a miracle. How does he do that？

他也是花了不少時間才體會到如果他還想活下去，他需要改變現狀，他需要改變他對生命的態度。書裡我最喜歡的一句話是 「到底要相信自己沒有手腳還是要相信自己潛力無限」他決定相信後者，既然等不到奇蹟出現，就把自己變成一個奇蹟吧！ 他是怎麼做到的呢？

First, he needs to learn to accept his condition and like who he is. Once he knows he needs to

首先他要接受自己的缺陷，當他學會愛自己，尊重自己之

love and respect himself, he is fearless and driven to success.

後，他就沒有什麼好擔心的了，可以盡全力去做到最好。

He is such an inspiration. I feel stronger and more confident towards things that I was too scared to try before. This book is highly recommended.

他的書很鼓勵人心，充滿了正面能量，看了之後我覺得我更有信心去面對我之前很恐懼的事。我很推薦大家去看這本書。

難忘的情境

請描述一個人生中難忘的情境

情境一｜畢業典禮 Graduation

在我大學畢業典禮上，我被選為代表畢業生對在校生致詞的代表，我很緊張因為我很容易忘詞。我做了很多小抄藏在手上，還好當天學校說可以拿個公文夾直接把稿子拿起來念。雖然有點緊張但是整體上來說還不錯，我自己也覺得很光榮。

情境二｜三分球 Three-point shot

高中很愛打籃球，常常下課就約三五好友打三對三。後來終於在高二選上校隊，高三那年的籃球聯賽，我真是出盡了鋒頭。本來兩隊不相上下，後來因為我的再見三分球我們拿到當年的冠軍，全場歡聲雷動，我一輩子都忘不了！

情境三｜上台表演出糗 School performance

國小為了慶祝母親節，學校都會舉辦歌唱比賽。音樂老師覺得我蠻有潛力了，所以就要我參加。平常練習的時候沒有什麼問題，可是正式比賽的時候我可能是因為太緊張，居然唱破音！雖然只有一段，可是我知道得獎是沒希望了。

情境四｜被女生拒絕 The rejection

高中時期我一直暗戀隔壁班的一個女生，我每天都跟她一起坐同一班公車到火車站，可是她並不認識我。有一天我決定要跟她告白，我鼓起勇氣去跟她說，可以跟你做朋友嗎？ 沒想到她看我一眼，搖搖頭，就走了！ 說真的如果時間可以倒轉，我絕對不會這樣做，實在太丟臉了！

情境五｜上廁所忘了鎖門 Lock that door

說起來真糗，那是我第一次坐飛機出國。我去上廁所，走進去關了門之後燈就亮了。我也不覺有異就開始弄我的東西，沒想到這時突然有人開門，是一個中年男子，他跟我都嚇了一大跳，他還跟我一鞠躬道歉再把門關上。我才驚覺我根本沒鎖門。

情境六｜偶像見面會 Meet and greet

我從國中就很迷郭富城，他是一個來自香港的明星，又帥又會跳舞。我上了高中跟同學一起參加他的歌迷會，一年有一次見面會。我們到了現場之後主辦單位給我們一人一個號碼牌，原來是抽出幾個可以上台拿親筆簽名，沒想到我真的被抽中了！ 可以近距離看他本人實在是畢生難忘！

情境七｜面對面 Face to face

幾年前跟同事到菲律賓浮潛，船伕説要帶我們到一個私人景點，水裡整片彩色的珊瑚從船上就可以隱約看的到，很像彩色的寶石！ 下水之後看到很多不同的魚種，突然間有隻獅子魚朝我游過來，我跟它四眼相對，又不敢靠太近怕被牠攻擊，那種感覺真的很驚悚。

情境八｜男友出軌 The cheater

出社會以後因為工作的關係認識了我的前男友，他是做業務的，口才很好。剛開始我也不覺得奇怪，只覺得他的工作很忙，常常找不到人。直到有一天他説要加班，我買了晚餐想拿去公司給他，卻看到他跟另一個女人很親密地從電梯走出來，我氣到想踹飛他。

Q 12 Please describe an unforgettable moment in your life.

MP3 48

請描述一個人生中難忘的情境

求婚 The proposal

I must say my proposal is an unforgettable moment in my life. I have been seeing my girlfriend for a bit more than 3 years, and I decided to ask her to marry me early this year. I have been thinking what would be the best way to do it. I decided to take her to the lounge bar she's always liked and asks her there.

說到難忘的情境，那應該就是我的求婚記了。我跟我的女朋友交往了三年多，今年年初我決定要跟她求婚。我一直在想該怎麼開口，我決定帶她到她喜歡的沙發酒吧，在那裡跟她求婚。

I wanted to surprise her, but I was getting more and more nervous when the time is approaching. The plan was, once we got seated, I will take out the ring and then ask her.

我想要給她個驚喜，可是時間越接近我就越緊張。我的計畫是等我們坐下來之後，我就把戒指拿出來。

I went ahead and made the reservation at the lounge, but the weather was really bad that day. It rained so much that it took us a long time to get there. She was a bit upset about why I insisted that we have to go out in such a bad weather.

我就照計畫去訂位，沒想到那天天氣很糟，雨下得很大，我們搞了半天才到。她有點不高興為什麼這種天氣我還要堅持出門。

Once we got to the lounge, I was so nervous, and I just got up and went to the toilet. I was trying to work up my courage, but I didn't realize I must have been in the toilet for a long time. She even sent a waiter in to check on me. I finally got back to the table, but the ring stuck in my pocket and I couldn't get it out. Then she already figured out what I was about to do. She burst into tears, and then yelled "I do ! "

我實在太緊張了，我們一到我就說要去廁所。我躲在廁所裡穩定我緊張的情緒，可是我應該是待了太久，她還叫服務生進來看看我有沒有事。我終於走回到座位上了，可是這個時候戒指卻卡在口袋拿不出來！ 看到這裡她已經猜到我要做什麼，沒想到她居然哭了出來大聲說"我願意！"

Although it didn't turn out as planned, it was still an unforgettable moment.

雖然跟我計畫的不一樣，可是還是真是個難忘的情境。

卡通/故事人物

請描述一個你喜歡的卡通或故事中的人物

人物一｜史努比 Snoopy

我一直都覺得史努比是全世界最幸福的狗，他有個好主人，還有一群好朋友。史努比整天躺在他的狗屋屋頂上幻想著不同的歷險記。他真的很有想像力，一下子是醫生，一下子是飛行員，雖然他的歷險記大部分都是失敗，但是他是隻不怕挫折的小狗！

人物二｜藍色小精靈 Smurf

藍色小精靈的樣子很可愛，大部分的精靈們都是藍色的皮膚，戴一頂白帽子還穿白褲，再加上配件。其中我最喜歡小聰明，他除了戴帽子之外，還帶了一副眼鏡，每次都有好主意！故事裡的壞巫師想盡辦法想把藍色小精靈抓來吃，小精靈們個子雖小，可是每次都會同心協力的度過難關。

人物三｜多啦 A 夢 Doraemon

我最喜歡多啦 A 夢了，他是隻來自未來的機器貓。他的外型像兩顆藍色的球上下連在一起，圓滾滾的很可愛。他的任務是照顧他的朋友兼主人大雄，大雄一天到晚出錯，還好多拉 A 夢身上有個神奇口袋，無論是什麼危急的情況他都可以拿出不同的法寶來幫他的朋友們解圍。

人物四｜白雪公主 Snow White

所有的公主裡面我最喜歡白雪公主的故事了，後母因為忌妒她的美貌，設計她吃下毒蘋果，好讓自己變成世界上最美的人。小時候只覺得還好她被王子解救了，長大之後我覺得這個故事根本就是社會的縮影，太出風頭是很容易遭人忌妒的！

人物五｜雪寶 Olaf

雪寶那活靈活現的樣子，我覺得他比冰雪奇緣裡的公主們都要迷人。他有一股不顧一切向前衝的勇氣，就像有夢想的年輕人。在故事裡，他一直期待夏天的到來，幻想著夏天有多麼的美好，因為他從來沒有經歷過，可是他沒想到一旦夏天到了，他可是會融化的！

人物六｜佩佩豬 Peppa pig

跟著我小姪女看卡通，我覺得佩佩豬很可愛，她的反應很天真，長大的志願是要當牙仙子。她有個弟弟，他們一家人很和樂，最大的興趣就是在下過雨的泥灘裡跳來跳去。我覺得小孩的童年就是要這麼單純，不像現在的童年充滿了電子產品。

人物七｜超人 Superman

超人真的是最經典的超級英雄人物，紅色的披風加上藍色的緊身衣，最特別的就是他的內褲外穿，還有胸前大大的 S，他的超能力讓他可以聽到世界各角落呼救的聲音。他不出任務的時候是個呆呆的記者叫克拉克，暗戀著一個叫露易絲的女孩。

人物八｜櫻木花道 Sakuragi

櫻木花道是一個搞笑人物，他因為一直被女生拒絕，有一天聽到他喜歡的女生說她喜歡籃球隊的人，櫻木花道就決定加入籃球隊。沒想到他實在很有天分，搞笑的他有一頭紅頭髮，常常以籃球天才自居！ 但是有沒有追到喜歡的女生，那又是另當別論了。

Q13 Please describe a character that you like from a cartoon or story.

MP3 49

請描述一個你喜歡的卡通或事故中的人物

海底總動員的多莉 Dory

I love Dory from Finding Nemo. Finding Nemo is a story about a clown fish which accidently got caught by human and his father searched everywhere he could trying to find him. The father clown fish named Marlin runs into Dory who helped him along the way to find his son. The duo went on an adventure across the 5 seas and finally found his son in Sydney, Australia. Dory is this blue fish with yellow fins, she suffers from short-term memory loss, but she never takes it as a problem！ I guess her memory is

我最喜歡《海底總動員》裡面的多莉，海底總動員是一個有關一隻小丑魚被人類抓走，而他的爸爸不停地搜尋只想找到他。這隻爸爸小丑魚叫馬林，他在途中遇到一隻叫多莉的魚，多莉沿途幫助他找他的兒子。這個兩人拍檔展開了橫跨五大洋的歷險記，到最後終於在澳洲雪梨找到他的兒子。多莉是一隻藍色帶有黃色鰭

just too short to remember it anyway !

的魚，她常常只有短期失憶症，可是她從來不覺得這是個問題。我想也是，因為她根本記不得她有記憶的問題！

Most people would think she is just a forgetful and careless fish. But I see her differently. I think she is the eternal optimist, she is always so happy and excited about things.

大部分的人會覺得她是一隻健忘又粗心的魚，。可是我不這麼想，我倒覺得她是終極的樂觀者！她對每件事總是那麼的正面，積極的去面對。

Her level of excitement is like she experiences things for the first time. I guess she is, because she couldn't remember she has done it before. Same as the frustration and disappointments, she doesn't hold things against anyone because she can't remember what they have said or done to

她對每件事的興奮程度就好像她從來沒做過這回事，我想也是，因為她不記得她有做過。同樣的，不高興或是失望的事她也忘得快，她對人沒有敵意，因為她早忘了別人是怎麼對

her any way. I guess it is probably not a bad thing to forget things that bother you after all.

她。我覺得忘記不好的事其實是件好事。

There is a sequel coming out about finding Dory this time. I am looking forward to seeing what happens after they found Nemo and how she got lost. I am sure it will be a great story !

海底總動員的續集要上映了，這次是有關尋找多莉的事。我很期待想知道他們找到尼莫之後多莉是怎樣不見的，這故事一定會很有趣。

名人

請描述一個你欣賞的名人

名人一｜歐巴馬 Barack Obama

歐巴馬是美國第一任民選的黑人總統，我覺得很有劃時代的意義。他除了做政治決定很果斷之外，他私底下的作風卻是非常的親民，就像隔壁鄰居一樣。美國總統是可以影響世界的人，但他卻不會看不起白宮的清潔工，我知道他會是一個以民意為重的人。

名人二｜周杰倫 Jay Chou

周杰倫的外表說實在並不出色，你大概不會用帥來形容他，只能說他很有型。他能有今天的成就真的是來自他寫歌作詞的天分，還有他獨特的詮釋方式。他也不斷嘗試，甚至在國際舞台都可以看到他大螢幕的演出，他的努力我們都看的到。

名人三 | 林志玲 Chi-Ling Lin

漂亮的模特兒很多，可是像志玲姐姐形象那麼好的還真不多。她很少有什麼負面新聞，又很愛做公益，常常幫慈善團體代言。她給人一種很溫柔但是又很堅強的印象，有誰不想像她一樣呢？ 如果她的歌藝再好一點，我覺得她當歌星的話也會有很多人支持。

名人四 | 林書豪 Jeremy Lin

林書豪真是台灣之光，就算我不迷籃球，我每次看到他有傑出表現的時候，我也會覺得與有榮焉，因為他從來也不會掩飾他是台灣人的事實，他也常回台灣看他的親戚還有家人。就算他在球場上表現不好，我也還是會為他加油。

名人五 | 成龍 Jacky Chan

外國人有哪一個不知道 Jacky Chan 是誰的？除了李小龍之外，我覺得他大概是外國人眼中唯一可以代表華人世界的影星了。因為他武打的背景，他其實沒有機會念什麼書，他為了演國際電影，努力地學英語，他的會話能力都是自學而來的，相當難得。

名人六｜郭台銘 Terry Guo

雖然郭台銘很早就將產業重心移到大陸去，對台灣來說不是件好事，但我卻不得不說他實在做得有聲有色。蘋果的訂單也全是他代工的，雖然民眾對他的評價很兩極，但畢竟他是個商人，他的重心就是賺錢，我很欣賞他做為成功商人的一面。

名人七｜希拉蕊 Hillary Clinton

雖然他的夫婿柯林頓曾經任職美國總統，可是很多人卻覺得希拉蕊表現得比柯林頓出色。因為她的律師背景還有政治經歷都不輸柯林頓，她也一直位居要職，曾經當過美國的國務卿。2016 年終於輪到她代表民主黨來選美國總統的大位。

名人八｜王雪紅 Cher Wang

王雪紅大家都不陌生，她是已故台灣經營之神王永慶的女兒，現在也是台灣的女首富。她也不是因為靠爸爸留下的家產而致富的，她一手創立宏達電子、威盛電子，沒有拿她爸爸一毛錢，卻有能力把台灣品牌 HTC 推向國際，她絕對有過人的判斷力還有執行力。

Q14 Please tell me about a famous person that you admire.

MP3 50

請描述一個你欣賞的名人

傑米奧利佛 Jamie Oliver

Jamie Oliver is someone I really look up to. There are lots of famous chefs in the world, but I think his belief makes him stand out from the rest. I think he is doing a lot of charity work through his ability to cook and understanding of food.

傑米奧利佛一直是我很欣賞的一個人，這世界上有很多出名的廚師，可是我覺得傑米的信念讓他與眾不同。我認為他是用廚藝的天分還有對食材的了解來做公益。

He knows everyone likcs to eat, but not everyone knows how to eat well or what is good for them. He just wants to promote the idea of eating good food to avoid being overweight.

他了解大家都喜歡吃美食，可是並不是每個人都清楚怎麼樣吃才是對健康有益。他想要推廣吃好的食物而不是讓人會肥胖的食物。

He wants to help to rectify the problem of being overweight in the UK when he noticed the number of people suffering obesity in the UK is skyrocketing.

他注意到英國過重的人口年年遽增，而他想拯救肥胖的問題。

He soon realized that, the most effective way to rectify the problem is to educate the future generation to stop the trend of being obese. He initiated a program to visit school canteens to inspire the food provider to offer nutritious food instead of the junk food to the kids.

他腦筋動得很快，他發現最有效的方法就是從教育下手，讓下一代不要加入肥胖的趨勢。他發起了到學校去拜訪福利社的食品供應商，讓他們避免提供垃圾食物，盡量提供有營養的食物。

At the same token, he wants to take this opportunity to educate kids about what type of food is good for them.

他也順便趁這個機會教育學生，讓他們了解什麼叫做好的食物。

I think Jamie Oliver is trying to change the world with his own power and wanting to make an

我覺得傑米奧利佛是想用他的力量來改變人們對食物的觀

impact on people's perception of food which is a wonderful thing to do. I know it is impossible to change things overnight, but at least he is raising awareness and trying to reach out to his viewers.

念，我覺得這是件很值得讚揚的事。我了解改變需要時間，他現在開始提倡這個觀念至少可以影響到他觀眾群的層面。

節慶

請描述一個對你來說重要的節慶

節慶一｜農曆新年 Chinese New Year

我小時候最期待除夕夜的到來，全家人可以一起圍爐吃年夜飯，小孩們還有紅包可以領。可是現在長大了，除了吃年夜飯，打通宵麻將之外，換我要給紅包，不只是那些姪子姪女，還有爸媽那包。如果年終領的不夠，還真的有點壓力呢！

節慶二｜元宵節 Lantern Festival

農曆年過後，高雄愛河燈會就登場了，愛河的兩邊沿岸裝飾著各式這樣的燈籠，配合河面的雷射水舞，真是美不勝收。我都會約朋友一起去，可是人真的好多，逛完再回家吃個湯圓就太完美了。我還沒有機會到平溪去看過天燈，應該要找一年元宵節去。

節慶三｜端午節 Dragon Boat Festival

端午節我最期待我媽包的粽子，她的粽子真是沒話說，都是真材實料。端午節都還沒到她就已經在準備材料。她一年就只做這一次，因為包粽子費時又費力，她年紀也大了。我從來沒去現場看過划龍舟，因為實在太熱了！ 偶而看看電視轉播倒還可以。

節慶四｜中秋節 Moon Festival / Mid-Autumn Festival

我最喜歡中秋節了！ 沖天炮聲沒有斷過，家家戶戶都在烤肉，滿街的香氣四溢真的讓人有種幸福感。可是天公不做美，中秋節前後常常遇到颱風，有時候颱風帶來的災害讓人不知道應該用什麼心情來面對人人慶祝家人團聚的時刻。

節慶五｜豐年祭 Harvest Festival

雖然我住在台北，離開部落已經很久了，可是如果豐年祭的時候我一定會找時間回去。對族人來說，豐年祭比過新年還重要！可是現在豐年祭好像變成地方政府宣傳觀光的手法，豐年祭的內容也變得像嘉年華會，完全失去了原有的意義。

節慶六｜復活節 Easter

復活節在台灣並不是很重要的節慶可是對我家來説倒是蠻重要的，因為我家是教徒。復活節的日期每年都不一樣，因為也是看農曆來決定。而且復活節我們家也不吃紅肉，只吃海鮮來紀念耶穌受難日。教堂也會舉辦復活節的彩蛋活動，讓小孩們了解耶穌重生的故事。

節慶七｜聖誕節 Christmas

在台灣雖然聖誕節有放假，可是卻不是因為聖誕的關係。我有參加教堂的唱詩班，聖誕前夕我們會到附近的教友家傳福音。平安夜時我家人們會一起去參加午夜彌撒，教會也會安排愛心活動到孤兒院去發聖誕禮物給小朋友，我覺得很有意義。

節慶八｜媽祖繞境 Ma Tsu touring parade

每年的媽祖繞境可是全台的盛事，每次繞境大概需要 7-8 天，我家人總是會查一下繞境的行程，希望有機會可以去鑽轎底祈求來年的好運。繞境的日期每年都不一樣，因為要擲筊來決定。很多政治人物也會參與，順便爭取信徒的選票。

Q 15 Please describe a festival which is important to you.

MP3 51

請描述一個對你來說重要的節慶

清明節 Tomb sweeping day

I would say Tomb sweeping day is quite an event in my family because we still got a few ancestors' plots in the cemetery where we go and pay our respects. One of the Tomb sweeping day tradition is to bring spring rolls as offerings.

清明節對我家來說還算是件大事，因為我們家還有幾門祖先的墓要去掃。清明節的其中一個傳統是要拜春捲。

My aunt will always prepare lots of food in her house, and the family will gather there for a big spring roll making spree before we head off to the cemetery. This is probably the only chance for me to catch up with my cousins and relatives from my father's side

我嬸嬸總是會準備很多材料，大家會先在她們家集合做春捲，做完再出發到墓園去。這也是一年中難得的機會可以見到爸爸那邊的表兄妹還有親戚。所以清明也

as well. So Tomb sweeping is also a social occasion for us.

是家族聚會。

Other than the spring rolls, we also need to have the gardening tools to get rid of the overgrown weeds, and also some ceremonial items, such as ghost money, incense sticks, and a set of colorful paper strips.

等我們做完春捲後，除了要準備園藝的工具來除掉高大的雜草，還需要帶祭拜用的東西，像紙錢、香，還有一疊彩色的壓墓紙。

We first do the general tidy up, and then we will put out offerings and set up the altar. When everyone is ready, we will light the incense sticks and burn the ghost money to greet our ancestors, to let them know their family is here to pay the respect and pray for good fortune.

我們首先會環境整理，再來把供品供桌弄好。等大家都差不多了，就點香燒紙錢向祖先膜拜，跟祖先說子孫們來看你們了，祈求祖先保佑。

The colorful paper strips are the final step of the ritual, they will be spread out evenly on the tomb and we will pin them down with

壓墓紙是最後一道步驟，我們會把彩色的紙用石頭一張張分別地壓在整個墳墓

rocks. It is kind of spooky because you have to literally walk on top of where the coffin is buried to pin the paper strips.

上，其實有一點恐怖因為你在埋葬棺材的上方走來走去。

The colorful strips served as the decoration to show the others that this tomb is properly looked after by their family.

壓墓紙算是一種裝飾，好讓別人知道這家的子孫有在照顧自己的祖墳。

雅思口語第三部分

學習進度表

□ Unit 01 Leader 領袖
□ Unit 02 Friendship 友誼
□ Unit 03 Food 食品
□ Unit 04 Education 教育
□ Unit 05 Gender 兩性
□ Unit 06 Tradition 傳統
□ Unit 07 Sport event 運動競賽
□ Unit 08 Advisement 廣告
□ Unit 09 Social media 社群網站
□ Unit 10 Accident 意外
□ Unit 11 Presents 禮物
□ Unit 12 Lifestyle 生活型態
□ Unit 13 Shopping 購物
□ Unit 14 Internet 網路
□ Unit 15 Travel 旅遊
□ Unit 16 Technology 科技
□ Unit 17 Emotion 情緒
□ Unit 18 Environmental issues 環保問題

是否能於考場中獲取理想成績？

★ 完成 12 單元 ▸ 可能
★ 完成 15 單元 ▸ 較有可能
★ 完成 18 單元 ▸ 一定可以

Leader

領袖

What makes a good leader?

優秀的領袖應該具備什麼條件

I believe a good leader should be strong and tough because sometimes the decisions he makes might not be acceptable to everyone. I also believe he needs to be able to listen to his people, and gather the information to make the most sensible decision.

我覺得一個好的領袖需要堅強也必須嚴格，因為有時候他們做出的決定並不是每個人都可以接受。我也相信他必須要能考慮人民的意見，綜合資訊而做出最適當的決策。

I understand the outcome might not be as expected every time, but he should own up to his mistakes instead of pointing fin-

我了解當然有時候結果不如預期，可是他也要有擔當的承認他的失誤，而不是

gers at others.

推託給別人。

Furthermore, integrity is also a key element, too. Because being a leader, he would be presented with a lot of temptations. It could be money, expensive presents or women even. If he doesn't have an integrity, I am afraid he will lose his way sooner than you think.

除此之外，清廉也是很重要的一部分，因為當你是個領袖，想想看會有多少誘惑送上門。有可能是金錢、貴重的禮物，甚至是女人。如果他沒有清廉的心，那他很快就會迷失方向。

Q2 Who is the leader in your family?

MP3 53

在你家是誰做主？

My family is a bit unconventional. I would say I am the leader by name, but my mother is the one who wears the pants. My mother registered me as the head of the family since my dad passed away. She just wanted me to inherit what is left from my dad.

我的家庭不是很傳統。我可以說我是掛名的領袖，可是我媽其實才是作主的人。在我爸過世之後我媽把我登記為一家之主，我知道她只是想讓我繼承爸爸留下來的一切。

My mother has never been a dominating person. She does not like to be put under the spot light, so she pushes me forward. My mother would actually ask my opinion when she couldn't come to a decision. I really appreciate how much support my mother gave me, especially being a single mother like her. She has al-

我媽從來不是個專橫的人，她完全不喜歡出風頭，所以家裡的事情都派我去處理。我媽下不了決定時還真的會來問我想怎麼做。我真的很感謝她那麼的支持我，當個單親媽媽不簡單呢。她一直都是我心

ways been the unofficial leader in my mind and always will be.

裡不過名的領袖，也永遠都會是。

討論話題字彙

單字	音標	詞性
❶ sensible	[ˈsɛnsəbəl]	形容詞
❷ element	[ˋɛləmənt]	名詞
❸ temptation	[tɛmpˈteʃən]	名詞
❹ integrity	[ɪnˋtɛgrətɪ]	名詞
❺ unconventional	[ˌʌnkənˈvɛnʃənəl]	形容詞
❻ inherit	[ɪnˈhɛrɪt]	動詞
❼ dominating	[dɔmɪneɪtɪŋ]	形容詞
❽ appreciate	[əˋpriʃɪˏet]	動詞

Friendship

友誼

Do you think it is difficult to meet people as you get older?

你覺得長大之後是不是比較難交朋友？

I don't think it is much more difficult I would say how you meet people is definitely different. When I was younger, I met all my friends through schools or neighborhood.

我覺得好像沒有比較難，可是我覺得交朋友的方式不同了。我年輕的時候，我的朋友全部都是學校的同學或是鄰居。

But as I get older, especially after I got into the workforce, I realized that my co-workers are my new circle of friends. I still meet new people other than people I

可是我長大了之後，尤其是進了職場，我發現我新的朋友圈就是我的同事們，除了同事我還是

work with, but most of them are either my clients or suppliers from work.

有交到新的朋友，大部分不是我的客戶就是我的供應商。

I am lucky enough to actually turn the business relationship into friendship with a few of my clients who are friends of mine now. I see them outside of work as well, we hang out now and again.

我算是蠻幸運地可以把工作的關係昇華成友誼，我有幾個客戶現在是我的好朋友，我們私下也會約出來，有空就見個面。

Do you think friendship would last forever?

你覺得友誼一定會歷久不衰嗎？

This is a hard question to answer, I would love to say yes, but deep down I know it doesn't. I think friendship is a two way street. Unless your friend also feels the same way and wants to keep the relationship going. Otherwise, it can end pretty quickly after not seeing that person for a while.

這是個很難回答的問題，我很想說是的，可是我心裡知道其實不會。我覺得友誼是雙向的，除非你的朋友也有同感，會主動地想持續下去，不然其實一陣子沒見很快大家就失去聯絡了。

I had this friend, she was always my best friend while we were growing up. We even went to high school together. I always imagine she would be part of my life even after I got married and had a baby. But for some reason we just stopped talking to each other after graduation. I guess we

我有一個青梅竹馬的朋友從小一起長大，還念同一所高中。我總是想說我結婚生小孩的時候她一定會在我身邊。可是很奇怪的是我們畢業後就漸漸不再找對方了，我猜是因為我們

were both waiting for each other to initiate and make the first move.

兩個都在等對方先主動聯絡。

討論話題字彙

單字	音標	詞性
❶ neighborhood	[ˈnebɚˌhʊd]	名詞
❷ workforce	[ˈwɜ:kfɔ:s]	名詞
❸ co-worker	[ˈkoˌwɝkɚ]	名詞
❹ client	['klaɪənt]	名詞
❺ imagine	[ɪˈmædʒɪn]	動詞
❻ graduation	[grædʒU\`eʃən]	名詞
❼ initiate	[ɪ\`nɪʃɪɪt]	動詞

Food

食品

Q1 Is Food safety becoming an increasingly serious problem in our lives?

MP3 56

食安問題逐漸變成我們生活中一個嚴重的問題了嗎？

I never thought food safety would even become a problem in the first place because food to me, is something that is safe to eat.

我從來沒有想過食品安全會成為一個問題，因為對我來說所謂食品都是安全無虞的，可以吃的東西。

Then after watching the news in the past couple of years, I was shocked by how much toxin we have been fed by those heartless,

但是在看過這幾年的新聞事件之後，我無法想像我們到底被那些沒有

profit driven food manufacturers. It makes me wonder how much more there is to be discovered.

良心，只愛錢的商人們騙著吃進了多少毒素。我在想還不知道有多少事件要爆發呢！

I really think law enforcement should take some responsibility, too. The current food safety regulation is full of flaws, and the inadequate punishment and sentence length do not reflect the seriousness of their crimes. The food manufacturers often walk out clean which is very disappointing.

我覺得執法者也要負點責任，目前的食品安全法規充滿漏洞，罰則根本不成比例，還有罰則太輕，根本無法反映出罪行影響的層面有多廣泛。食品製造商也常常無罪釋放，這太令人失望了。

Q2 What do you think of organic food?

MP3 57

你對有機食品有什麼想法？

Some people believe it is better for you and also better for the environment because organic farming follows a strict set of guideline on what pesticide and fertilizers are allowed to use. I don't know whether it is necessarily better for the health, but what really concerns me is the rising price of the grocery cost.

有些人覺得有機食品對身體比較好，也比較環保，因為有機耕種必須遵守嚴格的規定標準，尤其是農藥還有肥料種類的選用。我是不太曉得到底對身體是不是比較好，可是我的顧慮是物價的飆漲。

Organic food can cost up to 2-3 times more compared with food that was produced under the conventional methods. I would love to support the idea of organic farming, but I just don't think I can afford it unless my salary goes up to 2-3 times as well. Most of us grow up eating conventional

有機食品的價格通常是一般傳統耕種食品的2-3倍。我是很想支持有機耕種，可是我覺得除非我的薪水也漲2-3倍，不然我根本負擔不起。大部分的人都是吃

farmed food, and it doesn't seem to do us any harm.

傳統耕種食物長大的，好像也沒什麼不妥。

討論話題字彙

單字	音標	詞性
1 heartless	[ˈhɑtlɪs]	形容詞
2 manufacturer	[ˌmænjəˈfæktʃəɚ]	名詞
3 inadequate	[ɪnˈædɪkwɪt]	形容詞
4 disappointing	['dɪsə'pɔɪntɪŋ]	形容詞
5 increasingly	[ɪnˋkrisɪŋlɪ]	副詞
6 pesticide	[ˈpɛstɪˌsaɪd]	名詞
7 fertilizer	[ˋfɝtlˏaɪzɚ]	名詞
8 afford	[ə'fɔ:d]	動詞

Education

教育

Q1 What can school do to help students to be more prepared in the next stage of their lives?

MP3 58

學校教育對於學生面對未來的人生可以提供怎樣的幫助？

I think Taiwanese schools tend to focus on the academic performance rather than the industrial related training and knowledge.

我覺得台灣的學校都傾向專注在學業成績而不注重產業相關的訓練或是知識。

I chose to do the vocational training school instead where they provide more hands-on training than textbook learning. I still artic-

我反而選擇職業學校，因為他們會提供實際產業相關的訓練而不是死讀書。

ulated to university after I graduated.

I do think I have a better idea of what I want to achieve in the future compared with my friends who came through the conventional high school system. I chose to join the workforce instead of pursuing further studies because I actually felt I was ready to start working, and there is no need for me to obtain a master degree to do the things I want to do. I think the vocational training definitely helped me to know what I want to do.

我到最後還是上了大學，可是我覺得我比我那些就讀傳統高中的同學們更有想法。我後來選擇不去念碩士，而是直接就業，因為我覺得我準備好要工作了，而我想做的工作並不需要碩士學歷。我覺得是因為念職校的關係讓我知道我要什麼。

Do you think people are offered more opportunity in life if they have a qualification?

你同意學歷可以幫你打開更多機會的大門嗎?

Yes, I totally agree. I think qualification is a ticket of entry to all kinds of opportunities. That is something that makes you stand out from all those candidates who apply for the same job. How does the employer know who is best suited for the job before they even meet you？To be good on paper is definitely an advantage to push you through to the next round which is the interview. But, how well you can impress the selection panel and whether you get the job, that's another question.

是的！我完全同意，我覺得學歷是一張讓你通往很多機會的門票。學歷會讓你在一群申請同一份工作的應徵者中一枝獨秀。老闆在還沒見到你本人之前怎麼會知道你適合這份工作呢？所以有好的學經歷真的可以幫你爭取到面試的機會，可是你能不能讓考官們喜歡你，或者能不能得到那份工作，這又是另一個問題了。

When I apply for jobs, I often get calls for the interview. but I don't always get that job. That's what makes me realised if it wasn't for the qualification, I might not even make it that far.

說到應徵工作，我常常都會有面試的機會，雖然有時候我面試的表現並不好，這更是讓我深刻了解如果沒有學歷可能根本連面試的機會都沒有!

討論話題字彙

單字	音標	詞性
❶ academic	[ˌækəˋdɛmɪk]	形容詞
❷ articulate	[ɑrˋtɪkjəˌlet]	動詞
❸ obtain	[əbˋten]	動詞
❹ vocational	[voʊˈkeɪʃənl]	形容詞
❺ candidate	[ˋkændədet]	名詞
❻ advantage	[ədˋvæntɪdʒ]	名詞
❼ impress	[ɪmˈprɛs]	動詞
❽ realize	[ˋrɪəˌlaɪz]	動詞

Gender

兩性

Who needs to learn how to cook?Man or woman?

你覺得誰應該學煮飯，男人還是女人？

I know society expects women to take up the role of cooking in a household, but I personally believe men need to learn how to cook. Growing up as a girl I was coached by my mother to learn how to cook since day one, but my brother got away with doing most of the household duties. He was laughing at that time, but once we moved out of home, he quickly realised he doesn't even know how to do his laundry because my mother has always

我知道這個社會都期待女人來擔起煮飯的責任，可是我個人覺得男人才需要學煮飯。我是個女孩，而女孩們從小就會被媽媽帶在身邊學煮飯，可是反觀我哥哥幾乎什麼家事都不用做，他那時候可是爽得很。可是等我們搬出去的時候，他很快就發現他連衣服都不會洗，因為我媽從小

done it for him.

幫他做到大。

When it comes to cooking, I believe most men do not have a clue about basic cooking skills. I don't expect them to turn out to be Michelin chefs, but to know how to make a few stir-fried dishes would do them good.

談到煮飯，我相信大部分男生可能連最基本的煮飯技巧都不懂，我是不期待他們煮得像米其林主廚一樣好，可是會炒幾道菜對他們來說應該受用無窮。

What do you think of arranged marriage?

你對媒妁之言的婚姻有什麼感覺？

I think the arranged marriage here is not as strict as the arranged marriage in countries like India, a place where you might not even know the person who you will be married to. In Taiwan, It is more like meeting the potential life partner through a mutual friend or a professional match maker. Although you still get the family involvement, but you do have a say in deciding who you would like to marry.

我覺得在台灣的媒妁之言的婚姻不像其他國家如同印度一樣的嚴格，在那裏你可能完全不認識你將要嫁娶的人。在這裡比較像透過共同的朋友或是專業媒婆認識人。雖然這裡也會牽涉到家人的意見可是畢竟是你的婚姻，你還是有發表意見的空間。

I don't have anything against it as long as the couples are genuinely happy with each other and they both want to spend their lives together. I would hate to see an

我是不反對相親結婚，只要兩方面都是真心地想跟對方共度一生，我最不想看到的是其中有一方是

arranged marriage when one was forced to marry someone that he or she is not willing to commit to.

被逼或是對這個決定有疑慮的。

討論話題字彙

單字	音標	詞性
❶ expect	[ɪks'pekt]	動詞
❷ coached	[kəutʃt]	過去分詞
❸ household	['haushəuld]	名詞
❹ laundry	['lɔ:ndr]	名詞
❺ strict	[strɪkt]	形容詞
❻ potential	[pə'tenʃ(ə)l]	形容詞
❼ genuinely	['dʒenjuinlɪ]	形容詞
❽ commit	[kə'mɪt]	動詞

Tradition

傳統

Do you think wearing traditional costume is important?

你覺得穿傳統服裝很重要嗎?

I think it is important to keep the culture alive as much as possible, but a lot of traditions have become unpractical in the modern days. I think wearing traditional costume is one of the things that is disappearing fast because wearing a Chi-Pao is not fashionable, and not practical at all.

我覺得能夠盡量保持傳統是一件很重要的事，但是很多傳統到現在已經變得不合時宜。 我覺得穿傳統服裝是一件非常容易被淘汰的事，因為說真的穿旗袍真的沒有流行感，而且也非常不實穿。

I mean, how do you ride a scooter when you are wearing a

你看，如果穿旗袍你要怎麼騎機車

Chi-Pao？For that very reason, I think Vietnamese has done a great job, because their costume is actually practical, and it looks beautiful on the bike, too！That's why the traditional costume is still very popular in Vietnam.

I think if the designers can incorporate Chi-Pao with clothing of western design, it might make Chi-Pao more popular which might help us to keep the costume alive.

呢？從這個觀點來看的話，我覺得越南的傳統服裝就很棒，因為不只實穿而且就騎車來看還更美！所以在越南穿傳統服裝的人還是很多。

我覺得如果服裝設計師能夠把旗袍跟西式的服裝做結合，那旗袍的接受度會更高，這樣就更能延續傳統。

What are the traditions that you still practice at home? Why?

你們家有什麼傳統？為什麼要維持這個傳統?

One of the traditions is that we always stay up until midnight on Chinese New Year's eve and light the fireworks with my dad. In the old days, people believe the sound of the fireworks scares the monster away, which is the reason why we celebrate Chinese New Year.

我家其中的一個傳統是，我們除夕的時候都會守夜到午夜，然後跟我爸爸一起放鞭炮。傳說鞭炮的聲音會把年獸嚇走，這也是我們慶祝新年的由來。

I love this tradition not because it is to do with Chinese New Yearbut because because we get to bond with my dad, and we are always so looking forward to doing it together. Another tradition is to do with birthdays, my

可是我喜歡這個傳統的原因並不是因為過年，而是可以跟我爸爸一起玩的回憶，我們總是既期待又興奮。另一個傳統是有關生日，我媽堅

mother insists to make us pig knuckle noodle soup for our birthday. It is a tradition she grew up with. It just reminds her with our grandma.

持我們生日一定要吃豬腳麵線，這是她從小到大的傳統，她總是會想起我的外婆。

討論話題字彙

單字	音標	詞性
❶ disappearing	[ˏdɪsəˋpɪrɪŋ]	形容詞
❷ fashionable	['fæʃənəbl]	形容詞
❸ practical	['præktɪkəl]	形容詞
❹ incorporate	[ɪnˋkɔrpəˏret]	動詞
❺ midnight	[ˋmɪdˏnaɪt]	名詞
❻ bond	[bɔnd]	動詞
❼ forward	['fɔ:wəd]	副詞
❽ remind	[rɪˋmaɪnd]	動詞

Sport event

運動競賽

Q1 Do you think the Olympic is different now compared with ancient Olympic games?

MP3 64

你覺得原始的奧運跟現今奧運有何不同?

That's for sure, I believe the ancient Olympic games have a lot to do with the religion's beliefs and the importance of how it brings peace to all the Greece countries during the game.

絕對是，古代的奧運跟宗教神話很有關係，而且最難得的是奧運期間希臘所有的參賽小國都能和平相處。

I believe it is a lot more spiritual compared with the modern Olympic games. The intention of participating countries which take

我覺得古代的奧運比較有神聖的感覺，而且現在參賽國的動機已和原始的奧運不同。對於參賽國

parts in the games, definitely evolved. Nowadays, the countries are head over heels fighting for the opportunity to host the games. I believe it is all about bringing in profit for the local business and boost the tourism industry.

來說，所有的國家都爭著要當奧運的主辦國，我相信都是為了增加國家當地商業及觀光業的收入。

For the athletes, I think it didn't change that much. All they wanted is to win regardless what century it is. I think the modern Olympic is very commercially orientated.

對於運動員來說，應該沒有改變太多，因為無論如何運動員都是想拿金牌。我覺得現代的奧運非常的商業化。

What do you think of betting on sports events?

你對運動彩券有何感想？

I am not a big fan of gambling, and I would never bet on anything, let alone sports events. I believe anything with human involvement gets trickier when money gets involved, too. When an athlete did not perform as expected, it is hard to tell whether he just had a bad day or he was manipulated by someone.

我一直以來就不喜歡賭博，我從來沒有賭過什麼，更別説是體育活動。我覺得任何與人有關的活動一旦跟錢扯上關係就變得很複雜。當運動員今天表現不好的時候，很難判斷出他到底是單純的情況不好還是他被人控制。

I used to really enjoy watching baseball match, but ever since a whole bunch of baseball players got caught by foul play a few years ago, it really damaged the purity of baseball games. Some of players even got felony conviction and sent to jail which termi-

我以前很愛看棒球賽，可是自從一大群球員被爆出打假球的案子，這真的把棒球賽的單純性給毀了。其中一些球員還被定罪抓去關，球員生涯也因此斷了。我

nated their career as a professional player. I think betting on sports events should not even be legalized.

覺得運動彩券根本不應該合法。

討論話題字彙

單字	音標	詞性
❶ spiritual	[ˋspɪrɪtʃʊəl]	形容詞
❷ evolve	[ɪˋvɑlv]	動詞
❸ athletes	['æθli:ts]	名詞
❹ regardless	[rɪˋgɑrdlɪs]	副詞
❺ involvement	[ɪnˈvɑ:lvmənt]	名詞
❻ manipulated	[məˋnɪpjəˏled]	過去分詞
❼ conviction	[kənˈvɪkʃən]	名詞
❽ terminated	['tɜ:mɪneɪtɪd]	過去分詞

Advertisement

廣告

Q1 In what way have advertisements changed in the past 10 years.

MP3 66

過去十年裡廣告有怎樣的轉變?

I think advertisements evolved rapidly over the past 10 years due to the popularity of the smartphone. It is almost impossible to avoid advertisement these days because they are literally everywhere.

我覺得廣告因為智慧型手機的普遍性，在過去十年裡轉變很大。現在幾乎睜開眼睛就可以看到廣告，因為真的到處都是。

In the old days, they are mostly on TV, magazines, and even on my scooter when I only walked off for a few hours ! But nowadays, they are on my Facebook, LINE,

以前廣告大部分是在電視、雜誌或是機車上也有，就算我只不過離開幾個小時。反觀現

and Wechat, they follow me wherever I go. Not only that, I think the presentation of the advertisement has become more technology orientated as well.

在，臉書、LINE，或是微信上都有廣告。廣告好像追著我不放。不只這樣，我覺得呈現的方式也越來越高科技。

In order to draw the viewers' attention, the graphic designers use a lot of computer animation to make the advertisement stand out and make an impression on the viewer's mind. I think technology plays an important part in the advertisement evolution.

為了要引起觀眾的注意，視覺設計師會用很多電腦動畫來讓廣告引人注目，讓觀眾留下深刻印象。我覺得科技對廣告的轉變影響很大。

How do the advertisements influence you on purchasing an item?

廣告對於你決定購買某樣物品時有怎樣的影響?

I think influence is not a big enough word, I would say advertisements actually brainwash the viewers and detect what they buy. I'd like to pay attention on the latest product and the easiest way is look at the advertisements, Some of the advertisements are very cleverly done, after I watched them, I actually felt the urge to rush out of the door to buy it and try it out !

我覺得用影響來形容還不夠貼切，應該要說廣告直接幫你洗腦而且控制你的選擇。我喜歡注意現在有什麼新產品，而最容易的方式就是看廣告，有些廣告拍得很好，我看了之後會很想衝出門去買那個產品來試試看！

Although sometimes the products I bought did not demonstrate the desired result, I felt deceived, but there is nothing I can do ! The advertisement is feeding the infor-

雖然有時候有些產品實在是沒有廣告上講的神奇，我會覺得被騙，可是那也無可奈何。我只能說廣

mation to me, and I was convinced, that's all I can say.

告知道我想聽什麼，而且真的講到我的心坎裡。

討論話題字彙

單字	音標	詞性
❶ popularity	[ˌpɑ:pjuˈlærəti]	名詞
❷ literally	[`lɪtərəlɪ]	副詞
❸ presentation	[ˏprizɛn`teʃən]	名詞
❹ animation	[ˏænə`meʃən]	名詞
❺ brainwash	[`brenˏwɑʃ]	動詞
❻ attention	[ə`tɛnʃən]	名詞
❼ cleverly	[`klɛvɚlɪ]	副詞
❽ demonstrate	[`dɛmənˏstret]	動詞

Social media

社群網站

Q1 Do you think using social media poses danger in our lives?

MP3 68

你覺得使用社群網站對我們的生活有什麼潛在的危險嗎？

I think it is potentially dangerous because you have no idea who else has access to your profile other than your friends. What worries me the most is those people who like to update their location and activities in real time, it actually reveals more information than you think.

我覺得真的是有潛在的危險，因為你不知道除了你的朋友們，還有誰在看你的資料。其實最令人擔心的是那些喜歡即時上傳更新他們的所在地，還有從事的活動的人，這可是把你的行蹤都洩漏出去！

I know there is a privacy set-

我知道你可以更

ting function, but not everybody knows how it works. I was really surprised to find when someone shared your photo on Facebook, all his or her friends can see it, too. You just never know whether there is a predator out there waiting for his chance.

改隱私設定，可是不是每個人都知道怎麼改。當我發現原來如果有人分享你的照片，你朋友的朋友們也都看的到，我很驚訝！你真不知道是不是有壞人在等待機會害你。

What do you think of people who do not use social media?

你對於不用社群網站的人有什麼感想？

I understand life is all about choices and social media might not be everyone's cup of tea. I do respect their choice, but honestly, people choosing not to use social media are likely to lose touch with most people in their lives. Almost everybody owns a smartphone nowadays, and people with smartphones tend to use social media to communicate instead of the conventional phone calls. Even my 70-year-old grandmother can use Skype to call me !

我了解生活中充滿的選擇而且不是每個人都喜歡用社群網站。我尊重他們的選擇可是說真的如果他們選擇不用社群網站，很可能他們會漸漸地跟周邊的人們失去聯絡，因為現在大家都有智慧型手機，而且大家反而不用傳統的方式打電話，都用社群網站在聯絡。連我七十歲的奶奶都會用Skype打電話給我！

I often wonder what is the reason that makes them being re-

我總是在想是什麼原因讓人排斥使用

sentful about using social media and refuse to keep up with rest of the population. I guess they are not firm believers of selfies either; otherwise, I am sure they will be all over it!

社群網站而且情願跟其他人脫節。我覺得他們一定是不喜歡自拍，不然再多社群網站也不夠用！

討論話題字彙

單字	音標	詞性
❶ potentially	[pə`tɛnʃəlɪ]	副詞
❷ access	[`æksɛs]	動詞
❸ profile	[`profaɪl]	名詞
❹ reveal	[rɪ`vil]	動詞
❺ predator	[`prɛdətɚ]	名詞
❻ resentful	[rɪ`zɛntfəl]	形容詞
❼ population	[ˌpɑpjə`leʃən]	名詞
❽ selfie	[sɛlfi]	名詞

Accident

意外

Q1 Do you believe most accidents happened at home?

MP3 70

你覺得大部分的意外都是在家裡發生的嗎?

Well, I think minor accidents tend to happen at home like small cuts on the finger or bump on the head, but I must say things can go bad pretty quickly at home, especially when you have a young kid at home who needs adult supervision at all time. They could have drowned in the bath in a blink of an eye while the mother went to answer the door.

嗯，我覺得小意外大部分都是在家裡發生，就像不小心切到手，或是撞到頭。可是我必須要承認在家也可能出大事，尤其是家裡有小小孩需要大人不停看著的。媽媽可能走開去應門而已，一瞬間他們就在澡盆淹死了。

However, I do believe most of the horrific accidents happened outside of the house where we have less control of the surrounding, such as car accidents or shark attacks.

可是我相信大部分可怕的意外都是在戶外發生的，因為我們無法控制大環境，就像出車禍或是被鯊魚攻擊。

I know people are more alerted when they are out, but they also have less control of whether the car next to them is going to hit them !

我知道大家出門在外都會比較小心，可是就算小心也沒辦法控制旁邊的車要來撞他。

Do you think your government is fully prepared to deal with a catastrophic disaster?

你覺得你的政府有能力處理重大災難嗎?

Well, I don't think anyone can say they are fully prepared to deal with a catastrophic disaster because disasters always happen when you are least expecting it. And when you get caught off guard, sometimes you just panic and forgot how you are supposed to react in the practice run.

嗯，我不認為有人敢出來說他們有能力處理任何的重大災難，因為災難總是在人們沒有準備的時候發生。而當你毫無心理準備的時候，有時候你就慌了，根本忘了練習的時候是應該怎麼樣處理。

According to the past record, our politicians were not ready to deal with any kind of disaster at all. They were hopeless ! Those who are supposed to be working on the rescue plan were not even

從以前的紀錄看來，我們的一些官員是完全沒辦法處理任何災難，他們真的很沒用！那些應該坐鎮指揮救援的人都還沒

aware there was a disaster ! The rescue was always delayed and not well planned. Things have improved, but in a very slow fashion. Therefore, I wouldn't say the government is ready. All I can say is there is definitely room for improvement.

發現有災難正在發生。救援行動總是不夠迅速而且不夠周詳。現在是有好一點，可是進步的速度太慢。所以我不敢説政府準備好了，我只能説進步的空間還很大。

討論話題字彙

單字	音標	詞性
❶ drowned	[draʊnt]	過去分詞
❷ blink	[blɪŋk]	名詞
❸ horrific	[hɔˋrɪfɪk]	形容詞
❹ alerted	[ˋɔltɚt]	過去分詞
❺ guard	[gɑrd]	名詞
❻ politician	[ˌpɑləˋtɪʃən]	名詞
❼ suppose	[səˋpoz]	動詞
❽ rescue	[ˈrɛskju]	動詞

Presents

禮物

How do you pick the perfect present for someone?

你是怎樣決定哪樣禮物最適合某個人？

I think first I will observe the person's lifestyle and see if there is anything that he or she might need or something suits his or her lifestyle. Or I will try to have a conversation with the person and try to find out he or she likes without giving too much away.

首先我會先觀察那個人的生活型態，再看看他是不是需要什麼東西，還是有某樣東西他生活中會用得上的。不然我會試著在不讓他知道的形況下，跟他聊聊他喜歡什麼東西。

If they seem to have everything they need, and I couldn't

如果他什麼都不缺的話，而且我也猜

work out what they want then I will organise a surprise instead, like taking them to a restaurant and prearrange with the restaurant for the staff to jump out and sing a song for him or something.

不出他要什麼的話，那我就會安排一個驚喜給他，就像先跟餐廳串通好，然後再帶他去餐廳，再請服務生出來幫他唱首歌之類的。

I think a memorable moment is the best gift that anyone can ask for ! It doesn't have to be something tangible.

我覺得難忘的回憶就是最好的禮物，有錢也買不到！好的禮物不見得一定要是實體的東西。

Are there special customs regarding giving and receiving presents in your country?

在你的國家有什麼送禮的習俗還是禁忌嗎?

Yes, there are. Most of the customs are based on the rhythm of the Chinese words which could sound like either bringing a good fortune or cursing to the person who receives the present. For Example, you would never give someone a wall clock as a present because it sounds like attending someone's funeral in Mandarin.

有的，大部分的習俗跟禁忌都是跟中文的押韻有關，不是聽起來像吉祥話，就是好像詛咒收禮物的人壞事會發生。舉個例子來說，你不能送時鐘給人當禮物，因為中文聽來很像是送終。

Another interesting one is, never give an umbrella to your partner because it sounds like you will be breaking up with him or her. Taiwanese believes if a

另一個有趣的例子是不能送雨傘給男女朋友，因為有分手的意思。台灣人還相信孕婦不能碰尖的東

pregnant woman handles sharp objects such as needles and scissors would cause miscarriage.

西，像針還有剪刀之類的，因為會害人流產。

I know this is purely based on superstitious reasons and there is no scientific evidence to prove it, but please do not buy a manicure set for your friend's baby shower.

我知道這完全是迷信，一點科學根據都沒有，可是如果你朋友要辦孕媽媽寶寶臨盆前的派對，你千萬不要送她修指甲的剪刀組!

討論話題字彙

單字	音標	詞性
❶ observe	[əb`zɝv]	動詞
❷ conversation	[ˏkɑnvɚ`seʃən]	名詞
❸ memorable	[`mɛmərəb!]	形容詞
❹ tangible	[`tændʒəb!]	形容詞
❺ rhythm	[`rɪðəm]	名詞
❻ funeral	[`fjunərəl]	名詞
❼ superstitious	[ˏsupɚ`stɪʃəs]	形容詞
❽ evidence	[`ɛvədəns]	名詞

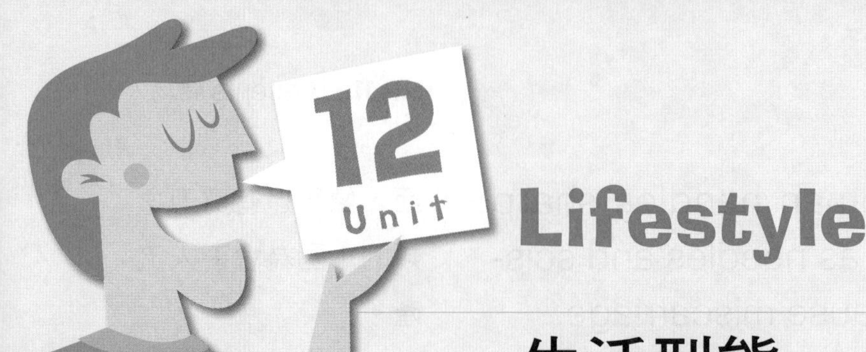

Lifestyle

生活型態

Q1 Do you consider your lifestyle healthy?

MP3 74

你覺得你的生活型態健康嗎?

I think my lifestyle is relatively healthy because I like to look after my body, eat well, and exercise regularly. I try to stay away from junk food as much as I can, like Fried chicken and burgers.

我覺得我的生活型態還算健康啦！因為我還蠻注意飲食跟規律的運動。我是盡量不吃像炸雞或漢堡之類的垃圾食物。

I always make sure I eat enough fruits and vegetables as well. I think what I eat is not a concern, but I do have a very bad habit which is to stay up late at night. I find it very soothing to just

而且我蔬菜水果會吃足量。我覺得我最大的問題不是吃，而是我喜歡晚睡的壞習慣。我很喜歡晚上一個人坐在那裏看電

sit there and watch TV alone at night. Sometimes I struggle to turn off the TV and go to bed.

視的感覺，很放鬆，放鬆到我有時候真的不想關電視去睡覺。

By the time I look at the clock, it would be 12:30, or 1 am even. I get tired quite easily, so I can't really say my lifestyle is 100% healthy.

等我抬頭看時間的時候，已經12點半了！有時候甚至已經1點了！我是蠻容易累的，所以我不能說我的生活型態百分百的健康。

What do you think is better for you?Home cooking or eating out?

你覺得怎樣比較健康?在家吃還是出去吃?

Ever since food safety became an issue in Taiwan, I am deeply convinced that home cooking is much better for you than eating out. However, I still cannot guarantee that home cooking is 100 percent safer because we still don't know whether the ingredients we bought from the shops were produced properly such as cooking oil.

自從食安問題在台灣延燒之後，我深深地相信家裡煮的東西是比外面的東西健康，可是就算這樣説，我還是無法保證家裡的東西是安全無虞的，因為我們不知道我們買回來的原料是不是好的，例如煮飯用的油。但是比起外面的東西，至少我們還能控制我們自己煮到底加了什麼東西進去。

But I guess I have more control on what is actually in a dish if

我可以保證絕對沒有防腐劑還有

I cook at home. I know it definitely doesn't have any preservative or artificial flavouring in it. However, home cooking is still home cooking. It is not restaurant quality food. I would still eat out because the restaurant food just tastes so much better. I am willing to risk my health once in a while!

人工調味料。然而，家裡煮的東西也只是這樣而已，真的沒有外面餐廳的水準。所以我還是會出去吃因為餐廳的東西真的好吃很多，好吃到我情願拿健康來冒險！

討論話題字彙

單字	音標	詞性
❶ relatively	[`rɛlətɪvlɪ]	副詞
❷ regularly	[`rɛgjələ-lɪ]	副詞
❸ struggle	[`strʌg!]	動詞
❹ ingredient	[ɪn`gridɪənt]	名詞
❺ properly	[`prɑpə-lɪ]	副詞
❻ definitely	[`dɛfənɪtlɪ]	副詞
❼ preservative	[prɪ`zɝvətɪv]	名詞
❽ artificial	[ˏɑrtə`fɪʃəl]	形容詞

Shopping

購物

Q1 Do you prefer to shop online or visit the stores?

MP3 76

你喜歡上網購物還是到實體店面去?

I actually like them both, but it depends how much time and how urgent I need the item.

我其實兩個都喜歡，可是要看我有多少時間或是我急不急著要那個東西。

If I had a lot of time and just trying to pick out something I want for a long time, I will browse online and compare the price and specification. I know it will take a few days at least for it to be delivered, but I can wait because I am in no hurry.

如果我有很多時間可以只是想慢慢挑一個我喜歡的東西，那我會上網逛逛比較一下價格跟規格。我知道送來要等好幾天，可是無所謂我不急。

However, if I need to pick out something at the last minute, say I just realised it is a friend's birthday, and I need a present for him today, I will definitely go to the stores. I know I might pay more in the store, but it doesn't leave me with a choice really.

可是如果今天是臨時需要一個東西，就好像剛發現朋友生日，需要一個禮物，那我就會去店面裡買。我知道可能會貴一點但是我也沒辦法。

How do big supermarket chains affect the local traditional markets?

大型連鎖超市對當地的傳統市場有什麼影響？

I believe big supermarket chains would impact the profit of the local small business vendors, such as corner grocery store, local butcher, fish monger which is most of the stalls you found in a traditional market. I must say most of the younger generation are drawn to chain supermarkets because it is a one-stop shop, they are very well stocked with a wide range of varieties, you can even get make-up items there, and inside the store is bright and clean inside which is opposite to the traditional market.

我相信大型的連鎖超市絕對會影響傳統市場攤商的生意，尤其是像一般的雜貨店，賣肉的，賣魚的攤販。我必須要說，年輕一輩的都會被大型連鎖超市吸引，因為超市裡什麼都有賣，各式各樣的選擇很多，就連化妝品也有，而且店裡面明亮又乾淨，跟傳統市場完全相反。

Without the younger generation's support of the local business, I think their business will really struggle especially when the younger generation start to take up the responsibility of cooking at home. The local market might not even exist by then.

如果沒有年輕一輩的來支持傳統市場，我相信攤商的生意會很難做，尤其是等到年輕的這批人開始擔起家裡煮飯的責任，傳統市場可能也不存在了。

討論話題字彙

單字	音標	詞性
❶ urgent	[ˈɜːrdʒənt]	形容詞
❷ browse	[braʊz]	動詞
❸ specification	[ˌspɛsəfɪˈkeʃən]	名詞
❹ at least	[æt list]	副詞
❺ vendor	[ˋvɛndɚ]	名詞
❻ monger	[ˋmʌŋgɚ]	名詞
❼ drawn	[drɔn]	過去分詞
❽ opposite	[ˋɑpəzɪt]	介係詞

Internet

網路

Q1

MP3 78

How does the Internet change the way that people have relationships with each other?

網路對人與人的交往有著什麼樣的影響和變化？

I don't know whether the internet has brought people closer or pushed us further apart because everything is just one click away, meeting or talking to people in person just seems like an idea of the past.

我不知道該說網路是讓人與人更靠近還是距離更遠，因為所有的事都可以上網處理。面對面的見面或聊天好像是過時的事。

I remember when I was younger I used to fight with my

我記得我小時候都跟我哥用Face-

brother through Facetime, and mind you, he was only upstairs in his bedroom ! But at the same token, I never really feel he was far away when he moved out of home to pursue further studies. We chat all the time online. I found it very comforting to be able to see him while talking to him.

time吵架，可是其實他就在樓上的房間裡。同樣的，當他因為讀書的原因搬出去的時候，我不覺得他離得很遠，因為我還是可以上網跟他見面聊天，讓我覺得有安心。

I guess we are now accustomed to talking to a flat screen than a real person in front of you.

我覺得大家應該很習慣對著平面的螢幕講話，反而不習慣跟人面對面聊天了。

Q2 Do you think meeting people online is a good thing?

MP3 79

你覺得上網交朋友是一件好事情嗎？

I don't see any harm in trying and honestly I think it is worth a shot especially when there is no other way to meet new people in the day-to-day routine. I know there are lots of dating sites or chat rooms where you can find people who are more like-minded or people who share common interests. I think all friendships have to start somewhere !

基本上我不覺得嘗試下有什麼不好的，因為如果每天固定的作息都沒辦法遇到其他人的話，那我覺得為什麼不試試看？我知道有很多交友網站或是聊天室可以加入，認識一些想法類似或是有共同興趣的人，友誼就是這樣開始的！

People seem to have this negative reaction when you told them you meet someone online. But I believe not everyone you met online is there to get you. It is no different than meeting someone in a bar. You still need to practice your

可是大部分的人如果聽到你說你們是在網上認識的，都會有種負面的反應，可是我相信不是每個人都是壞人。這跟在酒吧認識人沒什麼兩

common sense and be aware of the stranger danger regardless of where you meet them.

樣，反正不管你們是在哪裡認識的，你還是要保持理智知道面對陌生人要小心。

討論話題字彙

單字	音標	詞性
❶ upstairs	[ˌʌpˈsterz]	副詞
❷ pursue	[pɚˋsu]	動詞
❸ comforting	[ˈkʌmfɚtɪŋ]	形容詞
❹ accustomed	[əˋkʌstəmd]	過去分詞
❺ routine	[ruˋtin]	名詞
❻ like-minded	[ˋlaɪkˋmaɪndɪd]	形容詞
❼ common	[ˋkɑmən]	形容詞
❽ negative	[ˋnɛgətɪv]	形容詞

Travel

旅遊

Do you prefer domestic travel or international travel?

你喜歡國內旅遊還是出國旅遊？

I would prefer international travel if I can afford it, because going to a foreign country is very exciting, especially going to an exotic country like Brazil or somewhere in the Middle East.

如果我負擔的起的話，我會比較喜歡出國旅行。到陌生的國家總是很有新鮮感，尤其是那些異國風很濃的地方就像巴西或是某個中東國家。

The cultural and food are so different, just imagine you are in a carnival dancing with all the

特別是文化跟當地食物會很顯著的不同，想像一下你在巴

beautiful Brazilian girls or surrounded by the belly dancer while you are having lamb and flat bread.

西的嘉年華會跟那些美女一起跳舞，或是一邊享用著羊肉還有中東餅，桌邊被肚皮舞孃環繞著。

It would be a once-in-a-lifetime experience ! It is not something that you can experience in Taiwan. I would love to support domestic tourism more as well, but Taiwan is a small country, I think I have pretty much been to most of the tourist attractions anyway. It is just not as exciting as going overseas.

那些是一生難得的回憶，是在台灣感受不到的體驗。我也想支持國內旅遊可是台灣是個小國家，我覺得我好像大部分的觀光勝地我都去過了，真的沒什麼新鮮感了。

Do you prefer joining the pre-organised tour group or self-guided tour?

你比較喜歡跟團旅遊還是自由行？

I actually like the combination of both. I like to explore a new place at my own pace and interests. I will do my research prior to departure to work out a plan on what I would like to see and do once I get there. I will also research methods of transportation from point A to point B.

我其實喜歡混搭。我去旅遊的時候我喜歡照自己的意思走。我在出發之前會先做好功課，決定我到了當地之後想做什麼。我同時也會研究一下從A處到B處的交通方式。

If I get enough information and am confident about getting there on my own, I will go fully self-guided. However, in some places I will prefer to join the local tour because sometimes it works out more economically and other times it is just much easier in

如果我的資訊很充足，而且沒有什麼問題的話，那我就會完全自己走。可是有些地方我是會比較想參加當地旅行團的，因為有時候其實參加旅行團比較便宜，不

terms of transportation, especially those areas where there is no direct road to get there.

然就是交通上方便多了，尤其是想去那些很難自己可以去得到的地方。

討論話題字彙

單字	音標	詞性
❶ carnival	[ˋkɑrnəv!]	名詞
❷ surrounded	[səˋraʊnd]	過去分詞
❸ attractions	[əˋtrækʃəns]	名詞
❹ overseas	[ˋovɚˋsiz]	形容詞
❺ combination	[ˏkɑmbəˋneʃən]	名詞
❻ departure	[dɪˋpɑrtʃɚ]	名詞
❼ self-guided	[ˋsɛlfˋgaɪdɪd]	形容詞
❽ economical	[ˏikəˋnɑmɪk!]	形容詞

Technology

科技

Q1

MP3 82

Do you think people are spending too much time looking at their phones nowadays?

你覺得現代人是不是花太多時間在看手機?

It is a definite yes from me. I think I am guilty as charged. I find it hard to put my phone down, and I am constantly checking my phone to see if there is a message from someone.

沒錯，我就是這樣！我有時候真的沒辦法把電話放下來不看，而且我會一直拿出來看是不是有人傳訊息給我，我沒接到。

I must say I do get a bit sad if I don't hear from my friends for

我承認如果我朋友太久沒有傳訊息給

too long. It almost feels like I am addicted to my cell phone ! But the thing is, I know I am not alone, and most people are like me these days.

我的話，我還會有點失落感，可以說我幾乎手機上癮了。可是，我絕對不是唯一一個，大部分的人都跟我一樣啊！

The phone is not only a phone anymore, it is so versatile which can transform into anything. You can check your email, you can use it as a GPS, you can shop online. You name it!

手機已經不再只是手機了，隨時隨地都可以變成你想要的東西。你可以查你的電子郵件，你可以用它來當導航系統，還可以上網購物。你想得出來它就做得到！

How does technology help our lives?

科技對我們的生活有什麼幫助？

I think technology definitely makes our lives much easier or maybe I should say it probably made us lazier because it brought a lot of convenience to our lives. We take so much for granted compared with our parents' generation. I remembered my mother was telling me she had to go and collect firewood for the wood stove so my grandmother can cook in the kitchen.

我覺得科技的進步讓我們的生活容易很多，或是我應該說科技進步讓我們變得很懶惰因為它帶來了很多的方便性。比起我父母的年代，我們真的太不知道感恩。我記得有一次我媽跟我說她小時候需要去撿柴回家在灶裡生火，這樣我外婆才可以在廚房煮飯。

I guess we are the lucky generation, we grew up with a lot of technologies already in place such as telephone, TV, gas stove and microwaves. I am happy

所以我覺得我們真的是很幸福的一代，我們從小就對科技不陌生，有電話、電視、瓦斯爐還有微

about how technology has advanced. I cannot picture myself going and finding firewood to collect ! I don't think I will survive in that era.

波爐。我很慶幸有跟上科技進步的速度，我無法想像還要去撿柴的生活，我覺得我在那個年代應該活不下去。

討論話題字彙

單字	音標	詞性
❶ constantly	[`kɑnstəntlɪ]	副詞
❷ addicted	[ə`dɪktɪd]	過去分詞
❸ versatile	[ˈvɚsətəl, -ˌtaɪl]	形容詞
❹ transfer	[træns`fɝ]	動詞
❺ granted	[`græntɪd]	過去分詞
❻ generation	[ˌdʒɛnə`reʃən]	名詞
❼ advanced	[ædˈvænst]	過去分詞
❽ survive	[sɚ`vaɪv]	動詞

Emotion

情緒

Would you try to speak to someone when something troubles you?

如果你心裡有事的時候，你會找人談談抒發情緒嗎?

Well, I think mostly I will, but sometimes I just don't get a chance to. I know it is better for me if I can talk to someone and release some of the stress inside me.

嗯，我大部分時候會的，可是有時候我沒有機會。我知道找個人講一講抒發情緒對我比較好。

I don't intend to bottle up my feelings and keep things to my-self, but sometimes when I need someone to talk to, my friends

我也沒有故意要把情緒鎖在心裡不跟人說，只是有時候想找人的時候找我的朋

might be away or busy with their own life issues at that time.

友們可能不在，或是在忙他們自己生活中的瑣事。

And once that moment passes, I tend to just move on and not to think about it anymore. I don't really like when people start to give me advice on how to fix things, because honestly, I really just want someone to listen to me and let me blow off some steam !

當那個情緒過了我也就不再去想了。說真的，我最不喜歡旁人開始給我意見教我怎麼做。因為我只是想找個人聽我說，讓我發洩一下而已。

What will you do if you see people behaving badly?

如果你看到人有不好的行為，你會有什麼反應？

If it is something minor, like eating in a place that you shouldn't, I would be upset, but I might just let it go and not say a thing because it is not doing anyone any harm.

如果是小事，就像在不能吃東西的地方吃東西，我看到是會不太高興，可是我會當作沒這回事。

However, if it is a serious matter or someone's rights are being violated such as if I caught someone shoplifting or bullying others, I will do something but discretely. I find it hard to speak up in public; therefore, I don't think I will yell out at that moment, but I will definitely inform the shop owner or call the security guard.

可是如果是很重大的事，例如有人偷東西或是有人欺負別人的時候，我會有所作為，可是不會太張揚。我覺得我沒辦法在公開的地方大聲制止人，所以我當下不會大叫，可是我會跟店家或是保全說。

討論話題字彙

單字	音標	詞性
❶ mostly	[`mostlɪ]	副詞
❷ stress	[strɛs]	名詞
❸ issues	['ɪʃjʊz]	名詞
❹ advice	[əd`vaɪs]	名詞
❺ interfere	[ˏɪntɚ`fɪr]	動詞
❻ violated	[`vaɪəˏled]	過去分詞
❼ shoplifting	[`ʃɑpˏlɪftɪŋ]	名詞
❽ discretely	[dɪ`skritlɪ]	副詞

Environmental issues

環保問題

What can we do to slow down global warming?

我們可以怎樣減緩全球暖化的速度嗎？

People talk about reducing the carbon footprint a lot. Carbon dioxide seems to be the major contributor to global warming.

常常聽人家說節能減碳的概念，二氧化碳應該是全球暖化最主要的原因了。

I think there are a lot of things we can do as an individual, such as turning off the light when you are done with it, taking the public transportation or carpooling instead of driving on your own, or reducing the amount of rubbish.

我覺得我們可以盡一己之力的事很多，例如不用燈的時候就把燈關掉，搭乘大眾交通工具或是與人共乘，盡量減少自己開車，或是垃圾減量。

My favourite is tree planting. It would not only help reduce the carbon footprint, but also make the environment look nice. I know it seems very minimal how we can help to slow down the problem, but I am fully aware if we don't start doing something about it now, global warming would get much worst very quickly.

我最喜歡的是植樹，因為不只可以節能減碳，還可以美化環境。我知道對於全球暖化我們能做的事很微不足道可是如果我們不從現在開始做，全球暖化會來得又快又急！

How important is recycling?

你覺得資源回收很重要嗎?

I used to think recycling is just a way for some people to make a few extra bucks, because it is a time-consuming and labour intensive exercise to separate the recyclables from the waste. However, ever since I realised how much rubbish we generate every day and how little room we have to accommodate it, it totally changed my attitude towards recycling.

我以前覺得回收只不過是某些人想多賺幾塊錢的方式，因為要分類回收物既費時又費力。可是，自從我知道原來我們每人每天製造的垃圾量有這麼多而且可以處理垃圾的地方這麼少，我對回收的態度就改觀了。

I must say it is a common understanding that no one wants to live next to a rubbish tip, but not a lot of people realise how recycling would help us to reduce the needs for more rubbish disposal sites. I think recycling is one of

老實説，每個人都不想住在垃圾場旁邊，可是很少人了解資源回收可以減少我們對垃圾處理場的需求。我覺得回收是一個對垃圾減量最有效

the most effective ways to reduce the amount of the waste. It instantly turns the rubbish into gold!

的方式之一，立馬就把垃圾變黃金。

討論話題字彙

單字	音標	詞性
1 contributor	[kən`trɪbjʊtɚ]	名詞
2 carpool	[ˈkɑ:rpu:l]	名詞
3 carbon footprint	[ˈkɑrbən ˈfʊtˌprɪnt]	名詞
4 minimal	[ˈmɪnəməl]	形容詞
5 time consuming	[`taɪmkənˌsjumɪŋ]	形容詞
6 separate	[`sɛpəˏret]	動詞
7 accommodate	[ə`kɑməˏdet]	動詞
0 towards	[tɔ`wɔrdz]	介係詞

Learn Smart 073

猴腮雷 雅思口說 7+ 2 (附 MP3)

作　　者　陳幸美
發 行 人　周瑞德
執行總監　齊心瑀
行銷經理　楊景輝
企劃編輯　陳韋佑
封面構成　高鍾琪
內頁構成　菩薩蠻數位文化有限公司
印　　製　大亞彩色印刷製版股份有限公司
初　　版　2017 年 2 月
定　　價　新台幣 399 元
出　　版　倍斯特出版事業有限公司
電　　話　(02) 2351-2007
傳　　真　(02) 2351-0887
地　　址　100 台北市中正區福州街 1 號 10 樓之 2
E - m a i l　best.books.service@gmail.com
網　　址　www.bestbookstw.com

港澳地區總經銷　泛華發行代理有限公司
地　　　　　址　香港新界將軍澳工業邨駿昌街 7 號 2 樓
電　　　　　話　(852) 2798-2323
傳　　　　　真　(852) 2796-5471

國家圖書館出版品預行編目資料

猴腮雷雅思口說 7+2 / 陳幸美著. -- 初版. -- 臺北市 : 倍斯特, 2017.02 面 ; 公分. -- (Learn smart! ; 73)
ISBN 978-986-93766-6-2(平裝附光碟片)
1.國際英語語文測試系統 2.考試指南
805.189　105025547